Nobody's Inn

Key West

A Place to Die For

Wayne Gales

Photography by Tina Reigel

Conch Out Associates

For Tim

mi mancherai mio amico

Forward

Ah, here we are book number four. Bric's a little older but not much wiser (he still thinks too much with the little head). You would think running a bed and breakfast would be a dull job, but not for Bric Wahl, or I mean Russell Phillips. Ghosts, thieves, murderers, sexy MILFs, and a huge emerald and ruby-crusted gold cross keep things lively. Stay tuned.

I have a few people to acknowledge. Thanks to Bill Black, inspiration for my character Matt Black, for giving me excellent background information about the 1715 fleet that wrecked in a hurricane off Sebastian Inlet three hundred years ago. So far, millions in gold, silver, and gems have been recovered, and they estimate there are still over half a billion left undiscovered. Bill's out there nearly every day looking. Someday will be his day. Although the story is made up, Bill assures me it's possible.

Keep on keeping on.

In 2018 Tina and I sold our wonderful home in Tamarac, Florida, and moved a couple of hours north, to Melbourne, where she grew up. It's not far from the Sebastian area and the site of the 1715 wrecks. I've been inspired by those stories and it's become a big part of this book. The historical story is fascinating. Like most stories, truth is always better than fiction. You'll have to figure out where I blur the two.

I dedicate this book to my buddy Tim Hendrix, who sadly took his own life in 2017. He was the basis for my character Tim Heminger and was really an ex-CIA spook and spoke fluent Italian like a native, running the first Apple computer store in Turin, Italy, maintaining surveillance from a back room. I described him perfectly in the previous books, immaculately trimmed beard, three-piece suit, and polished shoes. And that was the choice of outfits for an off-road car race. I shall miss him dearly.

To my lifelong friend Karen Thurman, the inspiration for Karen Murphy, my love interest in earlier editions. She's my lover only on paper. In real life, my wife Tina and Karen are close friends. I kissed her hello once in friendship at Busch Gardens in Tampa. (My wife said "give her a kiss for me!") and it skeeved us both out.

The Brasher Doubloon is real. There are only seven in existence and I made up the eighth. Most recently one sold for over five million dollars. It's the rarest coin in America.

This book is a little shorter than my other three novels. I don't want to fill it full of fluff like other writers do. It's still a complete novel, but more like a series of vignettes than a complete story line.

I've been in the hospitality industry for more than forty years, and many of the stories are based on facts. You have to figure out which. As I have said before, Key West's fact is stranger than everyone else's fiction. Key West is just like any other normal little town.

Until it isn't.

Where do we go from here? Bric's getting old, and like Stevie Nicks said in a Fleetwood Mac song, I'm getting older too. I tried to kill Bric off at the end of this book, but my wife and Karen, who, in real life, wouldn't let me. Let's see where the road leads us. Enjoy

Wayne Gales

2024

1
I Don't Believe In No Ghosts

I don't believe in ghosts.

Nor do I believe in UFOs, or at least I don't believe in alien space ships with little green men. That being said, I'm quite positive that we are not alone in the universe. It's a vain creature that thinks he is the only intelligent creature among billions of galaxies that's capable of thinking, but, despite all the front page news on the grocery store tabloids, they don't visit us, abduct us, anal probe us, impregnate us, or slaughter our sheep.

I swear there ain't no Heaven but I pray there ain't no Hell.

I also don't believe in Bigfoot. As much as I love the concept of a whole other species of huge, cuddly furry hominids hiding out someplace in the Cascades, I'm pretty sure all those bearded rednecks in overalls and summer teeth (summer there, summer not) would have caught one or shot one, or got more than three seconds of blurry film on one by now.

I don't believe in the Loch Ness Monster, the Skunk Ape, or Ogopogo.

That doesn't make me a negative person; it makes me a realistic one. There are a lot of things I do believe in. I agree with most of Costner's rant in Bull Durham. I believe that Lee Harvey Oswald acted alone, I believe in soft-core pornography, chocolate chip cookies, opening your presents on Christmas morning rather than Christmas Eve, and I believe in long, slow, deep, soft, wet kisses that last for seven days.

I believe in those things too. But I don't believe in ghosts.

Correction.

I used to not believe in ghosts.

That is until I moved into a house full of em.

Apparitions. Things that go bump in the night, doors closing without help, cold spots in a room and things flying off tables, furniture rearranged in the dark so you do a Dick Van Dyke tumble walking a dark parlor with furniture locations you thought for sure you had memorized. All those things can be explained in a drafty hundred-and-fifty-year-old mansion, I guess but if you carry on a ten-minute conversation with something or someone you can see through, or worse yet, wake up in the middle of the night in the midst of, shall we say, and intimate moment, with someone - *something* - in bed with you, doing things that give teenagers wet dreams, well, that might change your mind. I hired one of those agencies that promised to rid any house of demons, ghosts, and spirits. They showed up with a complete Discovery Channel film crew. After two days of set-up, they turned all the mics, gauges, and cameras on - and got nothing. None of my "houseguests" made a showing, and none of the meters indicated a single speck of suspicious energy. They captured seven hours of a perfectly normal dark old house. The next day, disgusted, everybody loaded up and left, telling me not to call them anymore. As the last person slammed the front door, a kerosene lantern flew off the mantle, sailed across the room, and smashed itself against the wall. I distinctly heard laughter coming from upstairs.

But I'm getting a little ahead of myself.

When I got this wild hair up my ass to start up a bed and breakfast, I realized very quickly that my new name, provided by my ex-CIA sort of buddy and ex-SEAL mate, Tim Hemminger, would be hard put to get through the scrutiny required for things like home purchase and business licenses. I just couldn't produce enough of a paper trail to make title companies and title searchers happy. I had plenty of cold hard cash, but you can't just knock on a door and hand an owner a suitcase full of hundred dollar bills and get them to hand you a title. It all has to be done properly. With the help of my by-the-book, ultra-scrupulous straight-arrow lawyer uncle, Karl Wahl, we figured out a way around this, and legally. I sold something to my buddy John "Rumpy" Rumpendorfer for a tidy number with a lot of zeros at the end. I think I bought a pencil. Anyway, Rumpy had enough family investments in New Jersey that he was able to blend my treasure cash into his assets without making it look too obvious, so he could buy a house.

With dollars properly laundered legally, we started to look for a place and discovered that the old Sawyer mansion on Fleming Street had been put on the market after grandma Sawyer croaked. Yes, the very place where my late wife Wendy was born that kept popping up in various places in my life. We checked it out, had it inspected, poked, and prodded and all agreed it was in totally deplorable shape, way overpriced, and about to fall down. It was just perfect. Rumpy made an offer on my behalf and a month later we had a viable prospect for a classic Key West Bed and Breakfast.

So, renovations started. It didn't take long before we started feeling like one of those TV husband-and-wife couples that buy a place to renovate and flip for lots of quick cash, only to find out it needed a lot more work than expected. I thought a little paint and a few two-by-fours would get it up to code and we could hang a "Vacancy" sign out front. I figured no more than a hundred grand or so would get this place up to speed.

Wrong, it didn't get much past the porch. Dale Junior and I had some surprises in store, and we were only a few blocks down the street from each other. We were encountering similar problems but he had a cubic budget and a cable channel behind him to make a million-dollar home in Key West look like a three hundred-thousand-dollar home in Charlotte.

I didn't.

For one thing, the place was termite-ridden from top to bottom. If you sneezed on it, I bet it would have fallen down. I hired one of those fancy termite control companies you always see on TV in Miami to come down to tent and treat it. We must have killed forty-zillion little white bugs that week. After they left we started ripping out rotten walls, floors, timbers, cupboards, bathrooms, the porch, all the windows, and the widow's walk. Demo looks like fun and isn't. You have to wear a mask and hire burly men who drag their knuckles on the ground to do the heavy lifting. We blew through the hundred grand in the first week, and hardly scratched the surface. It's a miracle that the old cast iron, claw-foot tub that was sitting upstairs in the ancient bathroom didn't end up in the downstairs living room during the process. It was originally a six-bedroom mansion which hints it wouldn't be a huge problem to turn it into a six-room bed and breakfast, but it wasn't that easy. Fortunately, there were enough useless corners, blind hallways, and dusty alcoves that we were able to squeeze in a tiny bathroom for every unit, usable and a little bit bigger than what you find on an economy cruise ship. Along with the guestrooms we needed a crib for yours truly to crawl into plus a real kitchen. We tore out everything but the old cook shed that was attached to the back of the place. It was one room that was not termite-ridden and in fairly intact shape, but I didn't want to cook breakfast every morning roasting in a tiny outdoor room. Back in the day, the kitchen was built somewhat apart from the main house, mostly to keep the main building from burning down in case of fire, which was frequent, and also to create an open-air environment on an island with blistering heat and double-digit summer humidity. I told the crew to just wall it off and renovate around it to save money. I wasn't sure if the rest of the mansion needed major medical or minor miracle, but it became obvious that it wasn't going to be cheap. If I wasn't careful, we'd end up spending a little more than the annual budget of a small Central American country. As it was, we still ended up with all new electrical and plumbing, a fair amount of asbestos removal, and a complete installation of a sprinkler system and smoke alarms so we would meet the building code. A lot of effort went into making the old place look like an old place, with old-timey skeleton keys in every door, fake electric gas lamps and chandeliers in the rooms and hallways, and a lot of reclaimed shiplap on the walls, imported from those barn builder guys up north that you see on the DIY Channel.

The only thing that really got created modern-like was the kitchen, which was a state-of-the-art chef's dream room. We also installed a tiny elevator, hidden behind the stairway. It was small enough that you had to send people and luggage in one at a time. We also did a complete re-do of the back yard where the old carriage barn used to be and put in a kidney-shaped pool with a solar heater on the roof, a heat pump to keep the pool toasty during the winter, and a hot tub that would seat six cozily and ten if they were *really* friendly. It stayed at a constant One-oh-four, morning, noon, and night. It included a warning not to enter the tub if you have a heart condition, are pregnant, or have been excessively drinking. Hell, why would you want to get in one of those things unless you had *been* excessively drinking?

I tested that rule nearly every night.

For all intent and purpose, I was a "resident manager" and chief cook with a meat cleaver in one hand and a toilet plunger in the other. I even got a check every week for three hundred and sixty-three dollars so it all looked legitimate on the books, and was provided with a very modest room on the top floor. Just one double bed, a chair in the corner, and a lamp next to a big bookcase, plus French doors with access to the widow's walk, one private feature I didn't want to share, unless I had been drinking excessively and about to head for the hot tub with a human of the female persuasion.

Of course, that was just the part that was visible to the public. I had a whole other master suite hidden behind a bookcase that only the construction crew knew about, and at that, I made sure no crew member ever saw the whole thing complete. It had a big living room and my own little mini-kitchen with a side-by-side fridge. The freezer had two items – a gallon of Neapolitan Blue Bonnet Ice cream and two constantly full half gallons of Tito's vodka. I like my women hot and my vodka cold. The refrigerator side had every flavor of cranberry mixes and a container of Natalie's Orange juice that was replaced every week to keep it fresh on the rare occasion I didn't drain it first. There was also a nice master bathroom with a shower a bedroom with a king bed and a state-of-the-art entertainment center with speakers that could blow the house down.

Unfortunately, I could only crank up the music when all the rooms were unoccupied. It wouldn't look appropriate for the lowly hotel manager to have those kinds of digs so I kept it hidden to all. Unless you knew how to get in you wouldn't even know it was there. Oh, if someone got really snoopy and compared the inside building dimensions to the outside they would figure out something wasn't adding up, but up here on the third floor amongst the Royal Poinciana and banyan trees, it wasn't likely anyone would play amateur architect.

It was the perfect bachelor pad. I'm an atheist at a funeral; all dressed up and nowhere to go.

How did you access the room? Like I said, you got in through the bookcase. You could tug, pull, pry with a crowbar and shove that case as hard as you could and it wouldn't move an inch, unless you tipped over the Wyland blue acrylic dolphin on the shelf to the left, and pulled one specific book forwards. What book would I use to open a hidden room behind a bookcase? Ah, how about *The Diary of Anne Frank*, the Hebrew addition.

How appropriate.

Work progressed along at wallet-sapping speed, and the place was starting to look like a place. Then, one afternoon, the phone rang. I recognized the contractor's number, so I answered.

"Russell Phillips"

"Mister Phillips, it's Mark Williams, the contractor. I haven't been able to reach the owner. There's something he needs to see."

It wasn't any surprise Rumpy didn't answer the phone. For one thing, he really wasn't the owner, and anyway, this time of day he was probably rising with the tide, so to speak, on Marvin Key with a rum drink in one hand a semi-clothed blonde of questionable morals in the other. I wouldn't blame him if he didn't answer. Anyway, cell service is not that great out that way. He probably couldn't answer if he wanted to.

"The owner is otherwise occupied," I answered. "I can be there in ten minutes."

The inn was a five-minute walk from my apartment. I had taken over the little loft that Rio, rest her soul, used to live in until we got the Certificate of Occupancy at the B&B. I was looking forward to moving out of that phone booth. It was so small when you closed the front door the light went out, and the ceiling fan clipped the "Old Guys Rule" hat off my head almost every time I walked in and sent it sailing. I found Mark on the second floor of the mansion, standing next to a pile of rotten wood. I was a little surprised. At this point, I thought demolition was done weeks ago.

"What's up?" I asked. "I thought you were done tearing things apart. Find a problem?"

"Not exactly," he answered. "I was putting up some shiplap when I noticed that the wall in this room wasn't matching up with the wall in the other bedroom, so I took a peek with a crowbar. Sorry about the mess, but I guessed correctly, that there was a space between the walls." He pointed at the rubble. "I pulled a few boards off and found this." He motioned me forward. I stepped over the rubble and peered into the hole in the wall, but it was too dark to make anything out. "Here, use this," handing me a bright LED flashlight. Inside was a tiny recess. It was obvious the old wall to the bedroom had been boarded up for some reason. There wasn't much, a book on a table that looked like some kind of journal, an oil lamp, and a rickety rocking chair with the wicker bottom rotted out.

Then the flashlight illuminated something on the wall. It was an unfinished oil painting, covered in cobwebs and a coat of dust, but I could clearly see the subject, a portrait of a striking, beautiful, young, raven-haired woman in a low-cut green silk dress with her hair fixed up high on her head. A tortoise shell comb, Spanish style, held her hair up. But she wasn't the real subject of the portrait. Around her neck on a massive gold chain was a huge cross, probably six inches long and four wide, crusted with huge emeralds and a big ruby in the middle. It almost looked like something you would buy at a Halloween costume store for a buck.

But I was pretty sure it was real.

"What do you want me to do with this, Mr. Phillips?" Mark asked. I responded by reaching through the hole, picking up the journal, and easing the painting off the wall.

"Seal it back up," I answered. "I'll make sure the owner gets these."

"Exactly who is the owner?" He asked, "All I ever got was a number."

I thought quickly. "Nobody," I answered.

Just like that my little bed and breakfast had a name.

Flashback–The Beginning of Spanish Conquest in the New World

After Christopher Columbus "discovered" the new world, arguably centuries after Norsemen were believed to be the first Europeans to find North America and tens of thousands of years after the continents were populated from Asia by the people that would become native Americans, Spanish explorers began the systematic exploration and conquest of America, namely Mexico and Northern South America. The overseas expansion under the Spanish Crown of Castile was initiated under the royal authority and first accomplished by the Spanish conquistadors. The Americas were incorporated into the Spanish Empire, except for Brazil, Canada, several other small countries in South America, and the Caribbean Islands. The crown created civil and religious structures to administer the region with little or no regard for the indigenous occupants, whom they considered uncivilized savages. They encountered many cultures as advanced, if not more than any in Europe, but not possessing the same level of advanced technical military strength, including firearms, armor plating, cannon, and the use of a horse.

The motivations for colonial expansion were trade and the spread of the Catholic faith through indigenous conversions. "Spreading the faith" resulted in nearly the complete annihilation of every advanced civilization in the Americas, including Inca Maya, Aztecs, and many others, through forced slavery, war, and disease.

Although Columbus never actually set foot on Mainland North America, his voyages helped launch a wave of conquest in North and South America, the Caribbean, and control of a vast territory for over three centuries. The Spanish Empire would expand across the Caribbean Islands, half of South America, most of Central America, and much of North America, including present-day Mexico, Florida, and the Southwestern and Pacific Coast of North America. It is estimated that during this colonial period, a total of 1.86 million Spaniards settled in the Americas and a further 3.5 million immigrated during the post-colonial era (1850–1950); the estimate is 250,000 in the 16th century, and most during the 18th century as immigration was encouraged by the new Bourbon Dynasty.

Spain enjoyed a cultural golden age in the sixteenth and seventeenth centuries when silver and gold from American mines increasingly financed a long series of European and North African wars. Spanish wars of conquest included laying waste to much of the Netherlands and a disastrous attempt to invade England, finalized by the failed attempt of invasion by the Spanish Armada.

In the early 19th century, the Spanish-American wars of independence resulted in the emancipation of most Spanish colonies in the Americas, except for Cuba and Puerto Rico, which were finally given up in 1898, following the Spanish–American War, together with Guam and the Philippines in the Pacific. Spain's loss of these last territories politically ended the Spanish rule in the Americas.

The Spanish conquest of the Inca Empire was one of the most important campaigns in the Spanish colonization of the Americas. After years of preliminary exploration and military skirmishes, 180 Spanish soldiers under conquistador Francisco Pizarro, his brothers, and their native allies, captured the Sapa Inca Atahualpa in the 1532 Battle of Cajamarca. It was the first step in a long campaign that took decades of fighting but ended in Spanish victory in 1572 and colonization of the region as the Viceroyalty of Peru. The conquest of the Inca Empire in Quechua led to spin-off campaigns into present-day Chile and Colombia, as well as expeditions toward the Amazon Basin.

When the Spanish arrived at the borders of the Inca Empire in 1528, the empire spanned a considerable area and was by far the largest of the four grand pre-Columbian civilizations. Extending southward from the Ancomayo, which is now known as the Patía River, in southern present-day Colombia to the Maule River in what would later be known as Chile, and eastward from the Pacific Ocean to the edge of the Amazonian jungles, the empire covered some of the most mountainous terrain on Earth. In less than a century, the Inca had expanded their empire from about 155,000 square miles in 1448 to 690,000 square miles in 1528, just before the arrival of the Spanish. This vast area of land varied greatly in culture and in climate. Because of the diverse cultures and geography, the Inca allowed many areas of the empire to be governed under the control of local leaders, who were watched and monitored by Inca officials. However, under the administrative mechanisms established by the Inca, all parts of the empire answered to and were ultimately under the direct control of the Emperor. At its peak, scholars estimate that the population of the Inca Empire numbered more than sixteen million.

The son of the previous ruler, and the grandson of the Emperor, had commenced the dramatic expansion of the Inca Empire from its cultural and traditional base in the area around Cuzco. On his accession to the throne, Huayna Capac continued the policy of expansion by conquest, taking Inca armies north into what is today Ecuador. While he had to put down several rebellions during his reign, by the time of his death, his legitimacy was as unquestioned as was the primacy of Inca power.

However, expansion had resulted in its own problems. Many parts of the empire maintained distinctive cultures and these were at best resistive participants in the imperial project. The large extent of the empire, the extremely difficult terrain of much of it, and the fact that all communication and travel had to take place on foot or by boat seem to have caused increasing difficulty in the Incas' effective administration of the empire.

The Spanish conquistador Pizarro and his men were greatly aided in their enterprise by invading when the Inca Empire was in the midst of a war of succession between two princes. When both died suddenly in 1528 from what was probably smallpox, a disease introduced by the Spanish into the Americas, the question of who would succeed as emperor was thrown open. By 1713, the Inca Empire was in shambles as Spanish greed conquered the land and the people in an endless desire for natural riches including gold, silver, and emeralds.

Also known as Cerro Rico (Spanish for "Rich Mountain"), the peak's huge supply of silver has led to both immense riches gained by the Spanish invaders and appalling suffering by Native Americans.

Potosí was founded as a mining town in 1546, while Bolivia was still part of the Viceroyalty of Peru. Over the next 200 years, more than 40,000 tons of silver were shipped out of the town, making the Spanish Empire one of the richest the world had ever seen. But such vast wealth also came at a price. Thousands of indigenous people were forced to work at the mines, where many perished through accidents, brutal treatment, or poisoning by the mercury used in the extraction process. Around 30,000 African slaves were also brought to the city, where they were forced to work and die as human mules.

In 1672, Potosí became the site of the Spanish Colonial Mint and, with a population of around 200,000, was one of the richest cities in the world. But by the time Bolivia declared independence in 1825, the silver had largely run out, leaving tin as the main product.

To this day, a worker's collective extracts minerals from the mine. Due to the lack of protective equipment, the work is still very dangerous. Many miners die in cave-ins or from silicosis, a serious disease that damages the lungs, and there's been recent concern about the whole mine collapsing. Because of the hellish conditions, many of the miners survive by drinking extremely strong alcohol, chewing coca leaves, and worshiping Tio — a god of the underworld who holds the power of life and death between his fingers. El Tio, meaning "the Uncle," appears as a devilish creature, and his statues in the mines are frequently given offerings of cigarettes, strong alcohol, and coca leaves.

2
Who You Gonna Call?

From what I can tell, I have three ghostly residents – call them what you want: spirits, ghosts, apparitions, whatever. I've never believed in them and poo-poohed everyone that did, and bundled ghosts up with the aliens, flying saucers, Bigfoot, and the Skunk Ape. Now I have them for house guests, rattling around the hallways and stairs almost every night. Why only at night? I guess you have to ask the ghost union. Maybe they get double pay.

It took me a while but I finally figured out who was who. After some research and visiting the Key West Library to look at old articles and microfilm, along with reading grandma Sawyer's diary I found with the painting. I also spent weeks carefully going through Wendy's great-great grandfather's journal that we found sealed up behind the wall. Some old newspaper clippings were sandwiched inside the diary. I figured out two of them pretty quick. One, Louisa Sawyer was obvious. She was murdered right on the property. It was big news a hundred and fifty years ago. The owner, Wendy's distant ancestor, and Brody's namesake, Broderick Sawyer caught a guy, a big black gardener, with his pants down and Louisa with her dress up out in the carriage barn. Hubby was a lousy shot but apparently pretty good with a shovel. With his two-shot thirty-two caliber Derringer, Broderick Sawyer missed with the first shot but winged the lover on the second. He ran out of the barn and down the street out of sight (who says a man can't run with his pants down?), then the old man threw down the dead pistol, picked up a spade, and hacked his wife to pieces. Being the alleged lover was a man of color and Louisa was obviously a willing accomplice, it was considered a justified crime of passion and Broderick never went to trial. The whole incident was excused. Apparently, though, Louisa had some issue with the outcome as her ghost has decided to hang around ever since.

More about Louisa later.

Number two is an interesting story in itself. Albert Sawyer was a Lieutenant in the Confederate Army. Rumor has it he came to Key West with some gold bars that he sold to his great Uncle, the aforementioned Broderick Sawyer who was wealthy as a millionaire trader. The old man, head of this very house that I now own, noted Albert's visit in his log and that he paid Albert a large sum of money, discovered he had been scammed, and then later on figured out he had not been taken. I figured out that Albert had brought those very same gold-plated lead doorstops that got this whole saga going for me way back when. My first guess was that Broderick figured out he had been hoodwinked and dispatched Albert before he could flee town, but when you read the old man's log, which was carefully written despite the terrible spelling, and then read the microfilm of the Key West paper for the same dates, it notes an unidentified adult male was found dead about a half block from the Sawyer mansion three days *before* Broderick discovered his gold bars were plated lead. Just guessing, I suspect the old man arranged for his nephew's untimely demise and recovered his payment to poor Albert before he could leave town Anyway, it appears that Albert's ghost has been stuck here ever since, probably looking for the guy that whacked him.

I run into him occasionally, and so do my guests. He's not like Louisa, who often shows up fully visible and appears as a normal person, conversation and all, plus some fringe benefits. You only see Albert out of the corner of your eye, an image of a young man in a Confederate uniform, usually standing stock-still, his hand on the hilt of his saber, almost like a statue in a park, looking down the street, and never acknowledging you. He usually shows up at the most unexpected time and it's just enough to scare the bejeezus out of you.

The third spirit took me a little longer to figure out. He shows up very rarely, and seldom to me. Guests report an elderly man with a cane in a period three-piece white suit strolling along the balcony at night, a look-alike to Colonel Sanders without the chicken dinner. If you listen, you can hear the "clump, clump" of a cane. He seems to mind his own business but he does tip his hat to the ladies. It doesn't cause too much concern until people notice you can see the moon shining through him. It took me quite a while to figure out who it might be, and it wasn't until I read the end of Broderick's log, and the family diary that I found in the walled-off part of the bedroom before it came to me. Broderick Sawyer was documenting frequent encounters with two apparitions, a man and a woman back in about 1880. They were making things fly off shelves, blowing out lanterns, slamming doors, and making the old man's life miserable. Then suddenly, the log book ends in March of 1880. That's where I pick up the journal written by his son that reports the following.

"This morning we found father. He died in his sleep but I think not peacefully. His eyes and mouth were open and his hands were frozen in front of him in rigor mortis. I believe he was scared to death."

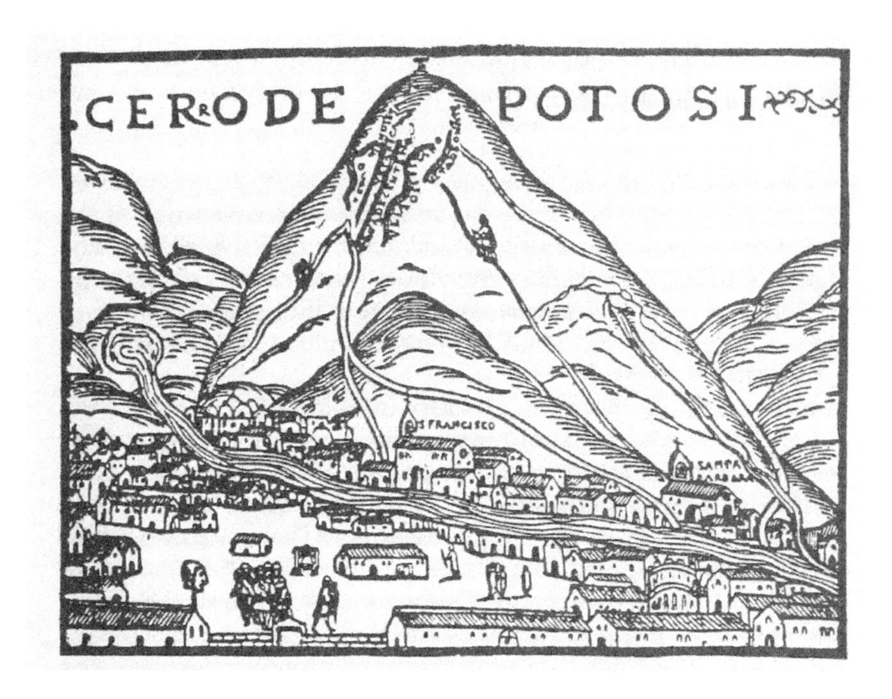
CERRO DE POTOSI
S FRANCISCO

Flashback – May 1713

Diego wasn't his real name. The *Conquistadores* couldn't pronounce it, nor did they wish to try, so they decided to name him Diego. Originally, one of the Incan Emperor's artisans, his leader, the Emperor, and most of his coworkers were either dead from overwork, torture, syphilis, or destined to perish deep underground in the Potosi mines, slaving under the stern and cruel eyes of the Spanish overseers. Working from dawn to dusk seven days a week, Diego slept on a bare dirt floor and was fed barely enough to stay alive, surviving on corn, squash, and potatoes, all foods that were native to the Americas. Despite his considerable skills, Diego's immediate boss, Juan deAlsama, still treated him like a savage. DeAlsama was actually comparatively kinder than most, and the beatings, which were frequent under his former boss, were less severe, and less frequent.

"I have a new project for you," Juan announced one day. Handing Diego a rough drawing, he motioned to the Indian. "They want you to make this for the new king's wife, Barbara of Portugal. I hear she's so ugly, maybe people will look at this cross instead of her face." Taking the crude drawing, Diego nodded vigorously, "I can make," he answered. "I need gold," and, holding up his left thumb "and some big nice emeralds about this size."

"You will have what you need," Juan growled. "The flotilla leaves for Spain in six months. Have it ready by then."

Diego nodded. After his master left him alone, he started his design. Glancing at the drawing, he began carving a large cross out of hardened and rendered beef fat, called tallow. Tallow was a valuable export item for candles, among other uses, but it was also useful for carving items that were to be cast in gold. A few days later, Juan came back to the room with two leather pouches in his hand. Throwing them to Diego, he growled again. "Best not lose them or steal any of it or you will join your friends at Potosi." Diego poured out the contents. In one bag he found, over a pound of pure gold nuggets and in the other, nine large emeralds. Hefting the gold, Diego exclaimed, "This is twice as much as I will need for one cross."

"Use what you need and give the rest back to me," answered deAlsama. He thought to himself *("Nobody else will know how much gold this will take, and I can easily sell the rest.")*

Then, reaching into another pocket, he threw the slave a third leather pouch. "Include this too in the cross," the Spaniard said. Diego opened the pouch and poured into his palm a magnificent red stone, already carved with facets. He looked up at deAlsama.

"I've never seen anything like this," remarked Diego.

"It's called a ruby," replied deAlsama. "It comes from far away, from a place called Burma. It was carried by a merchant from there to Japan, then by ship to the West Coast of Mexico, and then by mule to Valparaiso before it got to Columbia. It's probably the only ruby in this land. Add it to the cross."

Working every day, Diego carefully carved the cross design in the hard tallow. In ten days, he finished carving the cross in an ornate Spanish style, leaving indentations to secure the stones later. With the tallow cross nearly complete, he turned to the stones. Using a method not familiar to the Inca, but in the style of the Spanish *Conquistadores*, he carefully separated the emeralds so the best ones matched in color, were closest in size, and had the fewest occlusions.

Next, he attached each emerald to a wooden hardwood mandrill, split at the end to firmly hold the jewels, securing each one tightly with pitch. Then, a young boy using a bow wrapped one end around a wooden lathe. The Incas had been using the bow-operated lathe for thousands of years and never thought to fashion the bow into a weapon. The bow was pulled back and forth quickly to spin the lathe, almost as if he were trying to start a fire, spinning a grindstone that carefully ground facets on each emerald. Some of the stones had a faceted front that reflected light, and others were polished into oval cabochons in the contemporary Spanish style. While his *patrons* considered the designs beautiful, the Inca thought them disgusting. He carefully fit the real gems onto the wax model and then removed them again to prepare for casting.

He carefully pressed the tallow cross into fine wet sand,

pressing the sand around every niche, making an exact mold of the wax cross model. Next, he carefully placed a small, fired-clay cross in the center of the mold, balancing it with iron wire, thereby making the finished product lighter by leaving the inside hollow. Heating the pure gold to melting, over nineteen hundred degrees, he carefully poured the molten gold into the mold, watching the tallow cross he so painstakingly carved melt away in the process. He let it cool for four hours, and then knocked the sand away, prying the clay back out of the molded cross. Since the iron wire melted at a much higher temperature than the gold, his cross was pure. With a knife, he picked away any lose sand. Then with a leather cloth and earth, he polished the cross carefully. Near completion, he set the emeralds in place, bending the gold tines over to secure the stones. Finally, he placed the precious ruby in the center of the cross destined for the queen.

Wanting to please his boss, he used some of the remaining gold and hammered together a little snuff box, inserting some cuttings of the emerald chips on the lid. His work complete, he finished by taking a long length of hammered gold chain and strung it through the top of the cross. Smiling with satisfaction, he admired his work. "Here," he handed the masterpiece to Juan. "You like?" he asked.

"It will suffice," announced Juan, not admitting it was a beautiful piece of art. "I will send this to Spain. Ferdinand is so desperate for money, I wouldn't be surprised if he decides not to give it to that ugly bitch and instead sells the gold to pay his debts, but he loves her so much I'm sure he won't."

Diego then reached for a cloth-covered package and presented the snuff box to Juan. "A gift," he said eyes downcast. The *Patron* barely looked at the little box, shoving it in his pocket, grunting acknowledgment, but no thanks. This, he would keep for himself.

And Diego's rewards for creating such a beautiful cross? He didn't expect and received no thanks. That night, like always, he ate his cold soup, and he and his boy assistant curled up on a dirt floor without so much as a pillow or blanket, with grim satisfaction that at least they weren't sentenced to a slow agonizing death in Potosi. Correctly guessing his master would forget the unused gold, he hid it and the spare emeralds in the dust of his cell, secured away for the day he might be able to buy his freedom from a guard. He tried just that a few months later, only to have the guard pocket the gold and was thrown in chains and drug to the silver mines at Potosi, to be whipped daily before dying in a few short months of starvation.

3
Dogs have Masters. Cats have Staff

So, after many months and spending a butt load of money we were ready to open. I put ads in the Key West Citizen to staff a six-room B&B. I needed one housekeeper, two front desk/reservations agents, a groundskeeper, and somebody to relive me a day or two a week to cook breakfast. I did everything else; night audit, breakfast cook, human resources, and de facto inn keeper. Maintenance, beyond plunging a stuck toilet would be outcall, as would the pool service. The staff was easy to get. Good staff was a lot harder. I've been told if you could get a server to show up three out of five days they were eligible for Employee of the Month. So the ad went into the Citizen.

And nobody came.

I checked the paper.

Address right.

Number right.

Description right.

No bites, no calls.

Then I got word through the coconut telegraph. Nobody wanted to work here. They heard the house had been haunted for well over a hundred and fifty years. This was news to me. I wandered down to Bahama Village and hung out by the straw market for a while in the afternoon. Presently I saw a few locals, dressed in housekeeping uniforms; wander by on their way home from work. I approached several and offered work at twice the going rate. They showed interest until I told them what I was here for, and the location. They all shook their heads furiously and backed up with wide eyes and shaking heads. "I ain't gonna work dere don matter what you pay." And they would turn and walk away before I had a chance to utter another word. I can't both clean toilets and cook by myself. I had to find people.

The first solution came from my dear old friend. Scarlet, aka Kevin Montclaire, my six foot five, three hundred pound black cross-dressing friend came by one morning for coffee, tastefully dressed in multi-color stretch capri pants, shiny gold lamé top, and feathered platform heels.

"I never know what to call you," I started. "Are you a 'him' or a 'her'?"

"Oh mechanically, I'm definitely a 'him'" Scarlet explained. "I'm just a big black man in a dress, but," she went on. "I've come to identify more and more as a human of the female persuasion. Just like you, I like getting into ladies' underwear and eating pussy." She took a sip of coffee and smiled, "I guess I'm just a lesbian trapped in a man's body, but, unlike you, if a nice boy butt walks by, I ain't passing it up. You can call me girl, or she, iffn you wants. The way I see it, every name in the phone book's a potential date."

We talked for a while longer and I finally expressed my despair in being able to find help. "What you need?" Scarlet asked.

"Front desk, housekeeping, engineer, gardener, and someone to cook breakfast on my days off," I lamented. "As soon as I mention the location, they mumble about the place being haunted, and run away, no matter what pay I offer."

"Bahama Village people be leery of your permanent residents," Scarlet offered. "Have you thought about Eastern Europeans?"

"With my last venture, and all the drugs, prostitutes, and shady characters in that crowd, I prefer not," I shuddered. "People I don't like might come around, and somebody would end up dead. You remember how it ended last time." That wasn't a question, but a statement.

Scarlet nodded gravely and looked in her coffee cup for answers. Slowly she seemed to come to a decision. She put the cup down with decisiveness. "I'll be yo front desk. I tink a little ho-tel job would be fun, an a good change to my working nights at Aqua. I'm gettin tired o horny ol men grabbing my foam tits and not so fake ass." The big black crossdresser looked down at me, even though she was still sitting. "I can bring you staff," she ventured. "But they might look a little different."

"I need warm bodies," I responded. "No, not just warm bodies. I need competent people that work and won't steal me blind."

"Oh, they will work," Scarlet came back. "They a married couple. Tillie and Bela are both amazing friends and both looking for work. Want me to call them?"

"If they're out of work, how can they be any good?"

"They got pissed at the Southernmost GM and walked out one day. Let's just put it that they are a touch sensitive to their appearance."

I was curious about their "appearance", but decided not to ask. I desperately need staff. I didn't care if they had three heads.

"And a backup cook?"

"I can burn toast on any day you choose to be out of town, which, knowing you, will be infrequent. Actually, I'm a certified chef, with awards in New Orleans as long as my dick, which ain't no dainty thing. I cooked in the quarter for five years before moving to Key West, becoming an undercover cop and joining the crew at Aqua. I got u covered."

"Did you cook in a dress?" I held up both hands. "No, don't answer that," I said.

"Jes call me the black Martha Stewart but I own a hairbrush." She shot back.

"Think you can get that couple to meet me?" I ventured.

"No problem," Scarlet answered. "I'll have them here tomorrow morning first ting. Jes bring lots of dead presidents with you. Cash. And an open mind."

The next morning, I had a knock on the front door. I answered and tried not to look too surprised at the couple standing there, holding hands. "I'm Kovacs, Bela. In the USA, I would be Bela Kovacs. I'm from Romania." He blurted out his introduction like it was a canned speech, which it probably was. It brought to mind one of my favorite movies, and the next thing he uttered confirmed my thoughts. "My favorite movie is Forrest Gump." He blurted out. "People think he was stupid but he wasn't. Neither am I."

I shook his hand warmly. "Pleased to meet you, Bela." I turned to his wife, who was patiently waiting for her husband's self-introduction. It was obvious this was a common scene. "Hi," I reached for her hand. "Russell Phillips. Please call me Russell. Scarlet tells me you both have hotel experience."

"Matilda Kovacs." She thrust a diminutive hand into mine and returned my handshake. "Call me Tillie," she said with a little voice. Bela thrust his chest out. "I can fix anything, Mr. Russell and Tillie is the best housekeeper you will ever meet."

I considered the couple for a moment. "Scarlet highly recommends you both and that's good enough for me. Where did you meet Scarlet?" I asked. Matilda spoke up. "We used to work nights at Aqua and clean. They would let us come in early and watch the show. Scarlet was the only person that would talk to us because we looked different. We knew Scarlet was a man but she looks like a woman. She was nice."

I smiled in understanding. "Fourteen bucks an hour, most Mondays off, insurance included, and two weeks vacation a year. Paid."

Matilda smiled at the generous offer, much better than any other establishment in Key West has ever offered. "We don't take vacations, Mr. Russell," she said proudly. "If it's okay, instead of a vacation, you pay us an extra two weeks and we keep working. We're saving up to buy a house someday."

I looked at Bela. "The electrical is new, as is the plumbing, pool filter, heater, Jacuzzi pump, and all the kitchen appliances. Just keep everything working and we will all be happy." Bela nodded vigorously.

I had a team.

I guess there was one more member of the staff I needed only I didn't know it. One morning after opening the doors I heard the crunch of Rumpy's Four Runner on the gravel driveway. He stepped out and came in the back door. "What graces us with your visit?" I asked. "Out of rum at home?" Rumpy sat down at the reception desk, looking rather glum. Recognizing there was something serious going on, I asked. "What's wrong?"

"Crazy Willie died Sunday," he answered. "Massive stroke. After sixty years of smoking unfiltered Camels and downing a half bottle of Wild Turkey every day, it was bound to happen. No services," he continued. "Cremation and his ashes to be spread off Sunset Pier, according to his wife."

"I didn't even know he was married," I remarked. "I always thought he was tapping that bartender over at Schooner Wharf."

"Over twenty years," Rumpy answered. "Best kept secret that everyone in Key West knew but his wife. Every time he went to visit

Lilly, he told his wife he would be with Cousin Eddie. She never found out Eddie had croaked ten years ago." Rumpy coughed embarrassingly. "And he wasn't exactly lying."

"Wait a minute. You said Cousin Eddie was gone. How could he be telling the truth?"

"Ah, that's the reason I came by," he stood. "Wait here." And he walked back out to his car. Opening the door, the scruffiest old Golden Retriever with a dirty scarf tied around his neck jumped gingerly to the gravel driveway. Following Rumpy into the house, the dog walked up to me. Properly, I offered the back of my hand, which he carefully sniffed. Satisfied I wasn't a threat; he wagged his tail a half inch left and right and sat down. Rumpy announced. "Bric, meet Cousin Eddie, Willie's Golden. He needs a home, and every bed and breakfast needs a house dog."

"Oh, no," I answered, holding both hands up. "I have enough freeloaders to feed. The last thing I need is a dog."

"Pal, he needs a home and it needs to be in town," Rumpy answered. "He's no trouble, hardly eats, and never barks unless he senses danger. In ten years, Willie never spoke to him, pet him, bathed him, or paid any attention to him. He wouldn't be happy at my place out in the boonies. He's a genuine bar dog. His daddy probably gave Mike Mcloud the inspiration for his song. Everyone in town knows him and as long as that scarf is tied around his neck, signifying he belongs to somebody, nobody will ever turn him away."

"You've got the 'never bathed' part right," I remarked. "I can't even see the 'Golden' part of the retriever." Almost as if he understood the conversation, Eddie stood, stretched, and nosed his way out the back screen door. Walking up to the pool, he hesitated for a moment, and then nonchalantly walked down the steps to the shallow end. Using his bushy tail as a rudder, he leisurely took three laps, trailing mud like a New York barge dumping garbage before crawling back out and shaking violently, spattering dirty water over the entire backyard. Satisfied with the destruction, he plopped down on the deck. I suspect he was asleep before his head hit the bricks.

"See?" I pointed. "He has no business here. My maintenance guy will go nuts cleaning up after him. And the pool filter will be constantly clogged with dog hair."

"Job security for Bela," Rumpy answered. "He doesn't have anything else to do. Everything's new. Give him a little bath occasionally, and he will stay clean as a whistle," Rumpy promised. "I'll even come over once a week and brush him. It will be like he's not even here."

"Because he won't even be here," I answered. "No dogs."

"Just for a while just so I can find him a forever home," Rumpy answered.

I sighed in resignation. "You've done a lot for me over the years," I said. "Okay, just for a while. I suppose I'll need to go to PetSmart and pick up a food and water bowl, and some dog food." Before I changed my mind, Rumpy jumped up and went to his car, retrieving two stainless steel bowls and half a fifty-pound bag of dry dog food. "Supplement," Rumpy noted. "He will forage for most of his meals." For the first time in my memory, Rumpy stuck out his hand. "Thanks, pal. For once, I owe you. Trust me. You will grow to love him. Talk soon!" And with that, he bounded to his car and drove out of sight.

I leaned out of the front door to remind him this was a temporary commitment, but he was already out of sight around the corner.

4
Innkeeping

A Bed and Breakfast, is, by its own definition, just that. You run an inn, in this case, six rooms, and cook breakfast every morning. It sounds easy and isn't. There's always something. A clogged-up potty, a request for more bath towels, somebody raiding the kitchen at two a.m. for munchies, even though we're supposedly only a bed and breakfast. And there's the drunk and disorderly couple coming home in the middle of the night, waking everyone in the inn plus the guests in two hotels on either side, not to mention the occasional domestic dispute. They get one warning, and then they are uninvited to Nobody's Inn for the rest of their life. People learned pretty quickly if someone said put up or shut up, I would happily put up.

Peace reigned, or else.

"Bath time!" I invited Cousin Eddie up the stairs into my private quarters, and he climbed the stairs like a convicted criminal heading to the gallows. I stripped to my skin and dragged him into the shower; I washed the both of us three times until the water going down the drain was clear. You would have thought I was killing him. Thankfully it was a sixty-inch shower with a barn door, and he couldn't figure out how to escape. I toweled him off and he lumbered down the outside stairs the moment he was free, shaking violently all the way. Finding a spot in the sun poolside, he laid down to dry.

I wasn't qualified as an innkeeper. Remember just a few years earlier I was living on a derelict houseboat in the bay, sleeping on a filthy mattress with an ice chest as a fridge and no electricity. With that in mind, I surrounded myself with peeps that did have skills, and I just hung around looking important.

As for cooking, I did have some ability. After the Navy Seal stint, I worked on an offshore oil platform as an underwater welder. We had a full-time cook, but he managed to get himself killed in a fight over a hooker in New Orleans. He was found in the morning carved into pieces with a broken beer bottle. After that the boss decided to rotate the crew through the galley, each taking turns trying to poison everyone else every two weeks. I learned pretty fast to take extra duty, partially because my welding was only occasionally needed and partially to keep from starving to death or dying of salmonella. So, on my vacation, I enrolled in a New Orleans culinary college and learned both the fine points of breakfast and also became a pretty good Cajun/Creole chef, a talent I rarely have to use but enjoy. There's nothing like Jambalaya, conch fritters, etouffee, and Flaming Bananas Foster for dessert.

But that's another story.

My normal day looks like this: Up before four (we seniors never sleep much past then anyway), go downstairs to the kitchen, and check out the *menu du jour*. Turn on the radio quiet like and listen to Rude Girl and Molly Blue cut up. If we have good occupancy, I hang a menu on everyone's door the night before so they can check off what they want for breakfast, and the time they plan to eat between six and ten in the morning. If they plan to rise earlier than that they get a box with cereal, milk, fruit, and a granola bar, later than ten about the same or maybe they have to raid the fridge if I'm not around. If there are only one or two occupants in the inn, I usually find out what time they plan to get up and just prepare one meal.

Usually, I bake every day. There's banana nut bread, key lime muffins, or mango crasin-nut bread made every morning, fresh. I'm a messy cook and don't like to clean. Before starting her housekeeping duties every day Matilda, with the aid of a stool, cleans the kitchen and does the dishes, cussing me like a sailor every inch of the way, announcing to nobody in particular that the Muppet's Swedish Chef makes **a** smaller mess.

Bork Bork!

Other than hanging around all day and doing manager stuff, bookkeeping, payroll, and bills, my day should be pretty much done after breakfast, but I've created one other little function that I perform every night. Sometime around five p.m., Scarlet automatically brings out an ice chest full of beer and wines, sitting under a rolling cart with vodka, bourbon, rum, gin, whiskey, a blender on an extension cord, and a bunch of mixers, and we do my version of happy hour, maybe with a little cheese and Ritz crackers.

I know we don't have a liquor license, but I give it away, so it's just drinks with friends every afternoon, besides, I don't like drinking alone, and I like drinking. Besides, it's a good chance to entertain any single, decent-looking customers of the female species and get them oiled up a little. Since I can't roam Old Town without a serious disguise, I have the opportunity to mingle with the talent without the chance of getting caught by locals. Anyway, ATF has yet to show up at the front door with an assault weapon and a warrant.

Yet.

I'll burn that bridge when I get there.

Rumpy never found another home for Cousin Eddie, and after a few months, I really didn't mind. He was no real trouble, kept the stray cats from taking up unwelcome residence, and seemed to like it at the inn. I would swear he knew Willie was gone, and never attempted to sneak off to his old home. Aside from catching Hell from Bela for occasionally filling the pool filter with dog hair, (Rumpy never came by to brush him like he promised), he became a pretty good inn dog. Every morning after experimenting with the right location, he would adroitly lie down in the kitchen in the most inconvenient place in the room, so I had to step over him twenty times while cooking breakfast, then sneak off downtown every afternoon to supplement his diet, mooching hot dogs, burger patties or fish fingers at any one of a half dozen bars and always came home to sleep at the foot of my bed.

The rest of the time he practiced his favorite hobby; namely sleeping under Scarlet's feet at the reception desk

Flashback - July 1713

Juan carefully wrapped the jewel-covered cross in a leather cloth, and then slid it into a soft leather pouch. Hiding it in a coat pocket, he joined a party who made their way on foot from Potosi to the Spanish fort city of Cartagena, and on to the dock, where he met with Friar Accencio Rivera, who had just boarded the *San Miguel,* bound for Havana where it would become part of the Plate fleet. Taking the young monk to one side between buildings where nobody else could see them, he took the cross out of the bag. Showing it to the astonished friar, he instructed; "This is a necklace made for Barbara, newly crowned Queen of Spain, the former queen of Portugal." He handed the leather bundle to the Friar. "I trust you will deliver it personally. It's on the ship's manifest, but I don't want everyone to know of it, for I fear it could be stolen. I prefer it be kept by someone I know I can trust, a holy man like you."

The friar took the cross and fell to his knees, carefully examining the necklace in amazement. "It's beautiful," he exclaimed. "I'll wear it around my neck under my robes until we get to Spain and tell no one I have it. I will personally deliver it to King Phillip."

Juan put his hand on the priests shoulder. "I'm sure you will. The manifest does not say how it will be delivered, so please guard it with the utmost care. It's very valuable." The priest nodded understanding. He then brought out the little snuff box that Diego made for him. "I give you this." He told the priest, "Take it back with you on the ship. It will bring a much more handsome price in Seville. Sell it and give what you sell it for to my brother for safe keeping. I'll return some day and he can give me what it is worth in silver." The priest nodded knowingly. Fully a third of the treasure aboard the flotilla was undocumented. Four days later, the *San Miguel* and four other ships left Cartagena for Havana, Cuba, where they joined eight other vessels bound for Spain.

Juan watched the Treasure fleet sail with the tide, to Havana where the fleet languished for nearly two years before combining with other ships for safety.

5
The Golden Rule

It looked like it was going to be a cushy day for the cook. Three of the rooms were fishermen that left at o-dark-thirty. Last night I made them box breakfasts – scrambled egg/chorizo burritos (memories of Cabo San Lucas long ago), a banana, a box of OJ, and a granola bar. Room number Four was a couple that came in drunk and noisy at three a.m. I doubt I would see them before noon. That left me with the single lady in Room Six. Holly something, a mid-fifties Dallas executive, looking Milfy-ish at check-in when she threw a flirty glance my way and made me consider breaking my set-in-stone, unwritten rule – don't pork the customers.

Again.

Too often.

Holly wandered downstairs a little after eight, wearing a short terry robe that showed a generous flash of leg and I think not much else. She breezed past the kitchen and I rattled enough dishes to make her look inside.

"Breakfast?" I asked.

Holly stopped, flashed a twenty thousand dollar smile, and spoke in a Georgia drawl so thick you could cut it with a butter knife.

"Sug," that was her name for everyone, male or female. (Georgia-eze for sugar) "Gallons of coffee, for sure. I crawled a little too much Duval last night." She thought for a moment and continued. "Egg white omelet with skim milk cheese. Yogurt parfait with granola. Ah'll take it poolside if that's ok." And she headed out the door.

I raised my voice before the door closed. "Got all of that except the skim milk cheese. If you want to be that healthy, go vacation someplace like Tahoe. You're on the unhealthiest island in America. We're the unofficial headquarters of broken diets." I thought for a second and then added, "And freeze your ass off in that lake in July." After a moment's hesitation I added again, "And get arrested being outdoors in what I think you have on under that robe. Will you settle for some grated Swiss?" She waived her hand over her head in acknowledgment without looking back, slipped the robe off, and stepped into the pool. The "little else" turned out to be a pair of black lace panties that turned nearly clear in the pool. She was in incredibly good shape for her age, or for that matter, any age. I admired the scenery through the kitchen window and tried to not cut off a finger while I sliced tomatoes.

I arranged the omelet on a tray with the parfait and a pot of coffee, added a bud vase with one red rose, and kicked the back screen door open, with Cousin Eddie close behind to carefully watch for any food fallout.

"Breakfast is served," I announced and set the tray on a table poolside. I turned to walk back into the kitchen and she called out.

"Please, join me for coffee," Holly said, emerging from the pool un-modestly. Since it was there for the seeing (and likely the taking), I stood and admired the scenery. Full, seemingly natural breasts, unadorned by jewelry, tattoos, or piercings, no tan lines, and just enough tummy to announce proudly that she was somebody's mother. "I hate to eat alone," she said. I nodded and went inside for a cup. When I walked back out to the pool, Holly had her terry robe back on and was seated at the table tasting the yogurt. The robe was loosely open to the waist and as I pulled my apron off and folded it over the back of the chair, I couldn't help admiring the cleavage. At second glance, it was probably more expensive than the dental work. I sat down and poured myself a cup. We sat quietly for ten minutes while she devoured her omelet. For someone who didn't want to eat alone, there wasn't much conversation. I finally spoke.

"So how's your vacation going so far?"

"It's just what the doctor ordered," she answered over a mouthful of omelet. "I left my three-inch heels, hairspray, bra, panties, pantyhose, and most of my makeup in 'Lana. I really needed this trip, and your place here is real medicine." She took a sip of coffee and looked up. "And the people here, guests, help and," she smiled at me, "managers, are especially nice." I flashed my best 'charm the pants off her' smile. It was almost *fait accompli* at that point. "Oh, I'm just a nice guy with a few bad habits," I countered. I had her reeled in, fileted, and packaged at that moment. I would hazard we'd be in the sack by dark. She changed the subject again, trying vainly to play a little hard to get. "It's wonderful that you have hired the handicapped. That's very noble."

"Handicapped? Who?"

"Why, everyone that works here," she answered. "Yo housekeeper's a midget or a dwarf, depending on how y'all call 'em down here. The maintenance boy has Down syndrome, your gardener is a Negro with artificial legs and that nice lady at the front desk is obviously a man."

I stood up. "Holly, I don't know what you're talking about. I've known Scarlet for years and she's a fine human being, regardless of her choice of apparel. She has saved my life on more than one occasion, and I would gladly sacrifice my life for hers. Tillie and Bela are a very competent married couple with full-time jobs. Both are excellent employees. Marcus lost both legs while stationed outside of Kabul to an IED making sure you get to wear three-inch heels to work instead of a burka. If you ever saw him in uniform, he's got more medals on his chest than a Mexican general. He's an amazing gardener and his Key West Conch family goes back ten generations. Actually, rumor has it his ancestor was working here when he found his dick in the lady of the house and almost got it shot off. And to clarify, he's not a Negro. Marcus was born colored, became a Negro, then African American, and now he's just black. He's one helluva gardener. Nobody here is handicapped. They all pull their weight." And I turned to walk away.

Holly, embarrassed at the faux pas, called to me. "Hold y'alls horses. I wasn't trying to be disrespectful. I was *admiring* them, and." She hesitated and looked straight at me. "You" (If you throw a dog a stick he runs after it. Someone just threw me a T-bone. I was too smart to let my sense of propriety get in the way of a good roll in the hay.) I came back to the table and sat down. She hastily changed the subject. "Your residents are so nice too," she countered.

"Residents?" I asked. I suspected I understood what she meant, I guess I was fishing. (I wouldn't be happy till she threw her wet panties in my face.)

"Yes, you, of course," she said with a little come-hither Mona

Lisa smile. “And that nice Mexican lady, Louisa that I met last night.”

My eyebrows came up to act like I was surprised. “Louisa?” I asked.

Here we go again

“Oh yes. Nice lady. I got back about one and relaxed by the pool while I had a cigarette. I didn’t even notice her until she spoke to me. She must have been sitting in the shadows. We chatted for ten minutes or so. It was hard to understand her accent. Spanish or Mexican, or something I guess.” Holly finished her omelet and poured more coffee. She continued, “I didn’t ask, but it was obvious she had been at some sort of costume party. She was wearing a beautiful green silk dress. And,” she held her hand about even with her nipples. “Cut down to here, with her hair piled high in the back and held with a big tortoiseshell lookin comb. I thought those combs were illegal, or protected or something. And she was wearing a big cross with fake emeralds and a big fake ruby. We had a nice chat for a few minutes and then I reached down into my purse for another cigarette. When I looked back up, she was gone.”

I smiled, almost to myself. “Cuban,” I clarified. “She’s from Cuba, and I’m pretty sure those stones are genuine. Well, I hope she didn’t bother you too much.”

“Oh, Russell, not at all. She was wonderful to talk to. I want to know what room she’s in so I can go up and meet her again.”

“That’s not up to me. You never know when Louisa might drop in,” I answered.

“How can you say that?” Holly answered. “She has to live here. Why, there’s even a portrait of her hanging in the sitting room.” Holly stood up and took my hand. “Come here, I’ll show you.” I stood up, knowing where this was leading. We walked indoors and she led me to the sitting room. “There!” she pointed at the partially finished oil painting on the wall. “That’s Louisa. She was even wearing that same big gold cross, although heaven knows why.” She turned back to me. “I’m not sure why you are denying it, Russell. Please introduce me to her,” she pleaded.

I smiled grimly. I wasn’t sure how she was going to take this. I waved my hand toward the oil painting.

"Holly, please let me introduce you to Louisa Galarza Sawyer. Born in Havana, Cuba, October 2, 1842. Murdered on this property, just a few feet from where you had breakfast this morning on New Year's Eve 1879. She was brutally murdered in the carriage barn here, right where the pool is now, her head hacked off with a rusty shovel," I smiled again. "You see, she comes and goes when she pleases. Be glad she was pleasant. She's not always that nice to our guests, especially female."

"Why Russell, you're just pullin my foot," Holly answered, hands on her hips. "That weren't no ghost. Louisa was as real as you 'n me standing here. Don't call me a liar!"

"Well, next time she comes around," I answered with a smirk, "See if she will stand still for a picture."

Holly turned and walked away without another room, leaving the rest of her breakfast untouched. I had to smile. The Louisa story was one of my favorites, made even better for those guests that had a chance encounter, but not the only story.

While over-serving the guests every night, I played with my inner wish to be a comedian or a storyteller on nights when I had a pretty full house. I rotated five or six yarns every night at cocktail hour, mostly about Mel Fisher and the fabulous treasure found aboard the *Atocha* and *Santa Margarita*, and about some of the pirates, ah wreckers that were a part of my ancestral heritage.

One of my favorite stories, especially because it was just that – a story was steeped in legend that may or may not have been true. Told first by Bo Morgan a long time ago and embellished through the years by several old salts. I would stand by the pool and tell my yarn. With citronella torches lit around the edge to keep the mosquitos from dragging you off to a private place where they could suck you dry, I usually wore a black tee shirt with big letters MILF (Man I Love Fishing) on the front and proceed to drag out a tale that was originally only about four lines long. "In 1715 eleven ships sunk off the east coast of Florida," I would begin. "The survivors, while waiting to be rescued, amassed a huge hoard of gold, silver, and emeralds. Knowing it would probably be taken away from them when salvage ships arrived; they buried as much as they could on the beach, made a map on a thin sheet of hammered gold, and then screwed it to the shell of a huge leatherback turtle that was on the beach laying eggs.

Those leatherbacks can get as big as Volkswagens. They knew the turtle returned usually a couple of times a year, always in the exact same spot they were born. All that the surviving sailors needed to do was get rescued, wait till all the easy stuff was salvaged by other people, and then find their way back to the same beach. Then they would just camp out till the mother turtle showed up with the directions, and dig up the hidden treasure." I paused for dramatic effect, and then looked everyone in the eyes. "But as it turned out, nobody ever came back. They all ended up back in Spain or were captured or killed by pirates, or ended up dead from too much cheap rum." I paused again. "Not one single soul ever went back to that beach. That momma leatherback kept returning to her birthplace every year, year after year, with a treasure map to a cache worth millions riveted to her back. Legend has it she still does to this very day."

"Hey, that's impossible," retorted one guest. "Leatherback turtles live to be about fifty. Those ships sunk over three hundred years ago!"

"Are you spinning this yarn or am I?" I snarled back. "I'm only telling you the legend I've been told. Are you willing to go sit on that beach for six months and prove me wrong?"

Flashback - Two Years Later, July 1715

Normally, two fleets traveled between Spain and the Americas every year; the *Escuadron de Terra Firme* from Spain to South America, and the *Flota de Nova Espana* to Vera Cruz. Sometimes, these two fleets would travel together all the way to the Caribbean for safety from English privateers and pirates. The return voyage was more dangerous. The galleons were fully loaded with precious cargoes of gold, silver, jewelry, tobacco, spices, and indigo. The crews were tired and often plagued by health problems brought on by tropical diseases, malnutrition, and deplorable hygienic conditions on board. These conditions made ships even more vulnerable to attacks by pirates, but the greatest danger came from an uncontrollable element; the weather. The general weather conditions were more favorable during the summer months. The waters of the Atlantic Ocean were calmer, and the prevailing winds gentler. However, the very warm waters of the South Atlantic contributed to unstable weather and the then unpredictable rapid development of violent and devastating tropical storms called hurricanes.

As a result of France's Louis XIV policies of expansionism, Europe was ravaged by two major wars, between 1688 and 1715. These wars disrupted trade between the Americas and Europe, and Spain, highly dependent on the riches of the New World to finance her own policies of expansionism in Europe, suffered greatly. The first of these wars, the War of the Grand Alliance, ended in 1697 with the Treaty of Ryswick, but in 1701 another broke out, this time over the succession of the Spanish crown. Charles II had died childless, but on his deathbed, had named as his heir Philip, the grandson of Louis XIV of France.

Leopold I, the Holy Roman emperor, who wanted to see his son, Archduke Charles, ascend the throne, did not kindly receive this decision. Leopold also wanted to prevent at all costs any close alliance between France and Spain. War broke out, with England and the Dutch on one side, and Spain, France, Portugal, Bavaria, and Savoy on the other. The seas and oceans became the scene of naval battles and vicious encounters between merchant vessels and privateers. The sea routes between Spain and the Americas were no longer safe, and the vital flow of New World treasure was practically stopped.

Things were going badly for young Philip V and his kingdom. In the year 1702, Spain received a tremendous blow when a large English naval force entered Vigo Bay, on the northwestern coast of Spain. An all-out battle ensued, with the English fleet sinking a large number of warships, capturing others, and seizing a large treasure. The English sank another Spanish Treasure fleet in 1708, off Cartagena, Columbia, and in 1711 another one of Philip's treasure fleets was destroyed by a hurricane off the coast of Cuba. The War of Succession was finally ended in 1715 by a series of treaties known as the Peace of Utrecht. The treaty between England and France confirmed Philip V's succession to the throne of Spain, while Philip renounced his rights to the French throne. England was given Newfoundland, the island of St. Christopher, and the Hudson Bay territory. Although the war had ended, the peace was an uneasy one, and much friction remained between the former foes. At the end of this period of hostilities, Spain was in dire need of financial relief. At the King's order, a fleet was dispatched to America to bring back urgently needed gold and silver, which had been accumulating during the war. The eleven ships making up the fleet assembled in Havana in the summer of 1715. The fleet included the *Escuadron de Terra Firme*, which served South American trade routes out of Cartagena, and the *Flota de Nova Espana* which served the trade of Mexico and Manilla Galleons out of Vera Cruz, on the southeastern coast of present-day Mexico. The *Griffon*, a French merchant ship under the command of Captain Antoine Dare, was given permission to sail with the Spanish combined fleet. Now, everyone was busy getting ready for the long and treacherous journey back to Spain. Additional cargo was being loaded. Inventories were taken. Fresh water and food items were placed aboard each ship. After a two-year delay, the mighty Plate fleet was ready to sail home to Spain.

The *Escuadron de Terra Firme* was under the command of Captain-General Don Antonio de Escheverz y Zubiza, and consisted of six vessels. The Capitan-General was in direct command of the *Capitana,* the flagship, which was a captured English ship formerly named the *Hampton Court,* and was laden with a great number of chests of coins, gold bars, and jewelry, as well as tropical products. The flagship of the admiral, the *Almiranta,* was equally richly laden. The *Nuestra Senora de la Concepcion* carried gold coins and gold bars, as well as several chests of silver coins. The frigate *San Miguel,* the *El Ciervo,* and a patache, a smaller merchant vessel, completed the squadron.

The five ships of the New Spain Flota were under the general command of Captain-General Don Juan Esteban de Ubilla. Juan Esteban de Ubilla was himself on the *Capitana*, which carried some thirteen hundred chests containing 3,000,000 silver coins. There were also gold coins, gold bars, silver bars, and jewelry, as well as emeralds, pearls, and precious K'ang-Hsi Chinese porcelain which had been brought to Mexico by the Manila Galleons. The *Almiranta* carried nearly a thousand chests of silver coins, each individual chest containing some 3,000 coins. The *Refuerzo* carried eighty-one chests of silver coins and over fifty chests of worked silver. Another ship, a *patache*, carried some 44,000 pieces of eight. One frigate helped complete the Flota. The estimated value of the registered cargo of the combined fleet at 7,000,000 pieces of eight, which represented a real value of about $86 million in today's dollars

The fleet had suffered many delays and had been sitting idle for nearly two years. Pressure had been mounting for the fleet to sail. The Spanish crown was in dire need of money and so were merchants who had been unable to make their exotic goods available for sale on the European market. Under this tremendous pressure, Ubilla made the decision to start the long and perilous voyage back to the Old World, even though the hurricane season had long begun. This decision would prove to be fatal, for unknown to the Spaniards a tremendous and exceptionally powerful hurricane was brewing to the southeast of Cuba. The great Treasure fleet of 1715 sailed from Havana harbor in the early morning of July 24, a beautiful and calm day, with a gentle breeze to help the ships find the Florida current which ran north and up the Straits of Florida. Slowly and smoothly the ships of Ubilla's fleet gently followed the east coast of Florida, staying far enough away from the shore to take advantage of the Gulf Stream, and keeping clear of the treacherous shoals and reef formations that fringed the Florida coast. The first five days the voyage was uneventful with the weather remaining good and giving no indication whatsoever of the rapidly approaching killer storm. Then on July 29th, long swells started to appear, coming from the southeast. The atmosphere became heavy with moisture with the sun shining brightly through the haze. A gentle breeze still blew and the sea was smooth, but the swells started to make the ship gently dip and roll. Experienced navigators, pilots, and old hands started to be concerned. They knew that these were the early signs of an impending tropical storm.

The storm was traveling north, almost due east of the convoy, but still hundreds of miles away. The tropical cyclone had reached alarming intensity with winds at the center of the storm now reaching over one hundred miles per hour. By nightfall the hurricane had made a drastic change in course, suddenly veering directly to the west.

On the morning of July 30th, along the east coast of Florida, near present-day Sebastian, winds had begun to pick up and by midday had increased to well over 20 knots, and the sea was rapidly building. By late afternoon winds had increased to over thirty knots and the waves were reaching twenty feet. Ubilla's fleet was driven closer and closer to shore. The Captain General gave the order that all ships head into the wind to stay well clear of the reef and shoals but the attempt was only marginally successful. The velocity of the wind kept increasing, and by midnight, the ships were barely under control. Around 4 a.m. on July 31st, the hurricane struck the doomed ships with all its might, driving one ship after another on the deadly jagged reefs. The ships broke up like wooden toys. Ubilla's *Capitana* disintegrated, crushed on the reef like matchsticks. Almost all aboard were killed, including Captain General Ubilla. The entire fleet was lost, and of the some twenty-five hundred persons aboard various ships, over one thousand perished. For those who had miraculously survived, the ordeal was just beginning. They were stranded in an inhospitable land, infested with disease-carrying mosquitoes, rattlesnakes, wild animals, and hostile Indians, far from any European settlement. Two ships, the *Santisma Trinidad,* later known as the *Urca De Lima*, and the *San Miguel* washed completely over the beach in the storm surge and came aground in the Indian River. The *Urca* came aground in the Sebastian River, and the *San Miguel* bumped along the shallow bottom to the south of the present-day inlet and finally came to rest some two miles south.

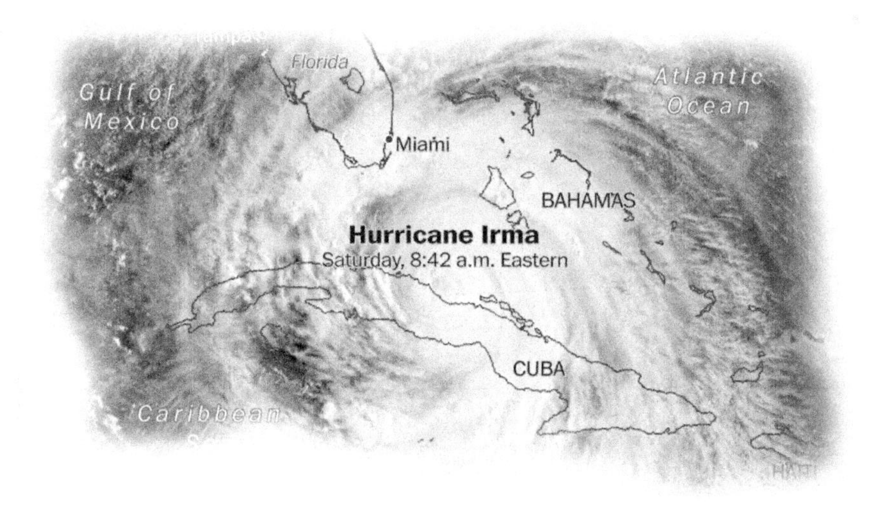
Florida
Gulf of
Mexico
Atlantic
Ocean
Miami
BAHAMAS
Hurricane Irma
Saturday, 8:42 a.m. Eastern
CUBA
Caribbean

7
Irmageddon

Every summer, keys people turn their eyes to the east and watch the weather channel a little more carefully. Rumors around town whispered that old wives' tale that the grotto at Our Lady of Lourdes had lost its mojo. The grotto was dedicated in 1922 and saw only Hurricane Donna in the 1960's supposedly keeping storms away, but superstitious residents felt it had its lost it's protection in recent years with Andrew, Georges, Mitch, and Wilma either hitting or affecting the keys, plus some other near misses. You started paying attention every summer, and now with NOAA getting their forecasting much better, you had five days to freak out instead of just three.

So we all watched with careful interest when a storm came off the coast of Africa and passed through the Cape Verde Islands. They named it Irma and it started heading due west. We had a lot of hope it would tear itself up over the mountains of Puerto Rico or Hispaniola, but no such luck. It reached Category Five and pointed right at us. Any idiot could tell it was going to hit *something*.

Our only hope it was going to hit the Bahamas and not us. Yes, I know if it hit Miami and Fort Lauderdale instead of the keys, the impact and cost would be ten times as much, but that wasn't *my* problem. I didn't own a bed and breakfast there; only here, so I rooted for a northern track, but by midweek it was apparent it would cross the keys someplace; most likely in the middle or lower part, so they issued a mandatory evacuation order, first for tourists, and three days later, all the residents. Naturally, I've never evacuated. I value my property, whether it be three shirts and a wetsuit on a derelict boat, or a multimillion-dollar mansion. I have no excuse why most of the rest of my gang stayed – no place to go and no way to get there I guess. None of my team had cars and even though I paid better than most, they lived hand to mouth walking to work or bussing every day, with any excess funds going down their throats on a Saturday night, or in the case of Bela and Matilda, in their savings nest egg. Scarlet didn't drink either and I have no idea where the money went. The moment they issued an evacuation order, she packed up and headed for the airport and away. "Heading for Nashville,. Gonna take in some country for a few weeks, besides there's a bass player named Jason up there that I've been Facebooking with. He plays five nights a week at Tootsies. I've been dying to tap that tight little butt for a year. I might just jump the fence for a few weeks."

Scarlet wasn't the only smart one. As soon as we got the evacuation order, Rumpy popped in. "Going to hole up with us?" I asked. "Not on your life," he answered. "Just dropped by to say adios. I'm outta here." He went on to tell us he boarded up his new house on Big Pine and was going to hightail it off to his brother Blotto's up in Jupiter. I guess he figured it was better to be safe than sorry. The little, but strong storm looked a lot more like it was going to hit up there than down here.

For the rest of the crew, including yours truly, it was stock up and hunker down. I headed for the Publix and joined the crowds for supplies, then by Conch Liquors for a few cases of vodka. With the tourists locked out, I could spend this storm safely in a Tito's fog. No need to board up. The house was just renovated with storm doors and hurricane windows. It was good for anything up to Cat Three – stronger than that it wouldn't matter anyway. This whole island wouldn't be much more than a concrete slab.

So we hunkered. And waited. It got windy Saturday afternoon and blew like hell Sunday. Power went out by noon and I only had local trees – poinciana, jacaranda, mangoes, and one big banyan, they only lost some branches, mostly it seemed into the pool. Those trees had survived more than one blow. At about two, I got my first knock. Bela and Matilda showed up with a little suitcase as wet as a couple of drowned rats. "Number Two – it's unlocked," I pointed. Within two hours my place was full of refugees, either staff or their friends. They figured I had supplies- no power, but neither did they. I had planned on drinking my vodka in peace, but not today.

Key West hardly got hit. A little wind, a little rain. Oh, we lost power for a few days, but that was to be expected. The city also issued a boil water order.

Who drinks water?

Up the keys, it was a different story. The storm surge topped six feet or more in some areas. Houses were flooded, almost every car drowned, and canals filled with crap from Big Coppit to Marathon. It tore the Hell out of Cudjoe, Summerland, Ramrod, Little Torch, Big Torch, and Big Pine. The wind pushed derelict boats and all kinds of garbage all the way into people's backyards and the middle of the Everglades You went to sleep with a couple of kayaks and woke up instead owning two Artic ice chests and an extra-large dog kennel. Like I said, the rock was spared much damage but it will be decades before the middle keys recover.

It earned a name that will be long remembered.

Irmageddon

One advantage – I had a big propane tank that was not only hooked up to the kitchen but also to the barbecue grill, so everyone could eat. I cooked and they all ate like vikings. We didn't have power so everything in the freezer thawed and had to be cooked. Matilda might have been a little over three feet tall but she could pound down a rib-eye that would have choked Shaquille O'Neal, and chase it down with two baked potatoes and a plate of navy beans. Bela came up a close second. Every night was the same routine; light torches around the pool, barbecue on the outdoor grill, eat too much, then drink too much, followed by a late-night swim. It was the only way you could cool off before crawling into a hot bed. With the torches out it was pitch black you didn't need to wear a swimsuit and nobody did. I didn't really care to see my staff skinny dipping, but it really wasn't any big deal and it was too dark to tell who was who. I'm glad Scarlet was out of town. The last time I saw a hose that big it was on the side of Key West Engine Number Four.

Four days later the lights same back on and the water started running, even though we still had to boil it if we wanted to use it for anything more than flushing. They didn't start letting tourists come for about a month, and by that time, all the businesses were up and ready to run, but almost starving to death. Oh, there were lots of parties for the locals, but there's just so much you can drink before your liver gives out, and you can't trade the same five-dollar bill back and forth before shops start to fail.

And they did. I'm glad this is a hobby and not a profession.

8
Kissin Cousins

One day a familiar classic white Porsche Targa pulled up. I couldn't mistake the bouncy flirt in the driver's seat and her demure, (although less so) sister in the right. It was Lex and Mary Elizabeth Sawyer, dropping by to check on their ancestral home. Boy were they surprised to discover that the old family mansion was now a bed and breakfast, and once inside, were astounded to see who was running the place.

"Uncle Bric!" they both shouted in twin speak and I was smothered in kisses, some of them not exactly uncle-ish. Scarlet looked on with abstract disapproval, while I untangled myself from both girls, "Shhh!" I put my finger to my lips. "Scarlet here knows who I am but nobody else does. I'm still Mr. Phillips, and will always be." I led them into the parlor, sat them down, and gave them the Readers Digest version of what had transpired over the past few years, leaving out the juicy parts, especially the part about nearly dying. I turned to Mary and continued, "So the last I heard, you were living on the west coast and engaged to some rich dude," I started.

"Oh, we got married," she answered, somewhat ashamed. "It lasted a whole three months until I discovered I didn't like him or for that matter, any other man." She smiled and looked away, quiet and confused. "Sissy likes pussy!" exclaimed Lex. "She's been working the field and passing the trash ever since!"

Mary blushed and looked down. "Not true," she answered. "I've been dating Casey for over a year. We're talking about getting married."

"Watch out for that dyke," Lex warned. "I gave her one sideways look one afternoon and she threatened to beat the shit out of me. Anyway," Lex paused, kissing her sister on the cheek in a rare gesture of filial affection. "It's okay. I've jumped the fence a few times, myself. It's no big deal. As they say, once you get over the smell, you've got it licked!"

Tactfully changing the subject, I motioned outside. "I thought you gave the Porsche away?" I said.

"What's a pack of penguins gonna do with a sports car?" Lex quipped. "It was sitting in a shed at the convent gathering dust when I got back. I found it about the same place I left it when I dumped the sheik or whatever he was. Six wives? Hell, I need six *men*. Anyway, I bought it back from the nuns for a song, threw in a new battery, gave it a wash & wax, and picked up where I left off. I thought a little road trip was what the doctor ordered, and here we are." She cringed, "Boy, don't ever drive through Texas in short shorts. That bible belt crowd will preach you right into the looney bin." She giggled for a moment, "Half the people want to 'save' you and the other half wants to get in your pants, or Sis's." Lex nodded toward Mary. "We couldn't get through Texas or Arkansas fast enough. My lips got sore blowing cops out of a ticket." She nodded toward her sister. "I brought sis along to keep me away from the ledge." Mary just looked down and nodded. She'd come a long way from her previous self, but she still oozed frump in her one-piece floral jumpsuit that ended six inches above her Birkenstocks. Lex, on the other hand, was still, er, Lex. She was poured into a pair of tattered cutoff blue jeans with a fair amount of butt cheek showing, a short yellow tube top under a white long-sleeved sheer blouse totally unbuttoned and tied at the waist, and a cute little hat, pushed back until her straw-colored hair framed her angelic face. There was nary a tan line in sight, at least the parts I could see and I would guess everywhere else.

"So, what are your plans?" I asked.

"Mary wants to cruise the south end of Duval Street past the pink triangle and scout for talent of the female persuasion," Lex replied. "For me, I shouldn't have any trouble finding something to do." She smiled and stared straight into my eyes. "Or someone." I returned the look with an even stare and a silly grin. Things were different now, and I had confirmed long ago we weren't even related. Now she was just a young, very sexy blonde without a lot of willpower. And even less won't power.

Maybe, just maybe I might tap that now, especially after Holly labeled me a kook and flew the coop without saying goodbye.

There isn't an angel of conscience sitting on my right shoulder, nor a girlfriend cramping my style. We'll have to see how developments develop.

I got them checked in and then as an afterthought, wrote a name on a piece of paper and handed it to Mary.

"Rude Girl aka Rudy Gee was one of my best friends ever. Rudy and her 'SO' Molly are Local DJ's and she MC's at the tea dance at La Te Da on Duval Street every Sunday. Rude Girl thinks I'm long gone, so just tell her that a good friend gave you her name and she will be happy to introduce you around. She's well-connected with the lesbian community. I listen to her almost every morning while making breakfast. You won't meet a nicer human."

Mary vaguely nodded thanks and quickly jammed the slip of paper into her back pocket without looking at it.

"Well, in the meantime Unc, ah Mr. Philips, were gonna grab some rays and hangout for a while by the pool. We'll see you out back in a little bit."

I nodded and left them with a heads-up. "You're welcome to stay as long as you want, free of charge, but if you do, ah, you might run into some of my permanent residents." I briefed them on the three ghosts. Mary looked a little frightened, but Lex brightened up. She became about as animated as I ever saw her. "Ghosts!" She cried, suddenly excited. "Really? I'm a confirmed Medium. I've been to a dozen séances at the Winchester House of Mystery in San Jose California. More than once I freaked out the fake ghost hunters when I conjured up a real spirit. Perhaps the apparitions and I will have a chance to meet and chat a little."

The girls retrieved what little they brought with them out of the front bonnet of the Porsche and vanished upstairs to their rooms. A while later, they emerged poolside. Mary was wearing a one-piece that would have been perfect in a Coca-Cola ad on the back page of a 1932 National Geographic, and she looked like she could survive a flak burst. Some things just never change. Lex also was wearing a one-piece.

The bottoms.

She walked out in every bit of thirty cents worth of dental floss that probably cost more than a house payment. It wasn't meant to cover the playground but to draw your attention *to* it. One thing for sure, Lex still didn't have a follicle of hair below the neckline. You've heard of a camel toe? This was the whole camel.

We dropped into a routine after a few days. Lex came home every night, sometimes at dusk for "happy hour" and sometimes just before breakfast, but she always came home – alone. She occasionally knocked on my door for a nightcap and we went downstairs. I often thought of my Titos stash in the other room but never took her in the Fortress of Solitude, as Scarlet started calling my man cave. There are some things, even someone who was once to be thought a niece, shouldn't find out about. Did we do it? There are also some things even my readers don't need to know either.

Mary came and went. She never brought anyone home, but Rudy must have done a good job introducing her around as she was sometimes gone for days. She's a big girl and can take care of herself. I wish her the best.

Pass the trash? Who's passing who?

One night, we were relaxing around the pool, me in cargo shorts and tee shirt and Lex in one of my tee shirts and thong panties. She just about nearly almost barely managed to cover all the important parts, but not too successfully. Like she really cared. I asked if she had met the residents.

She took a pull from her drink, lit a big fat joint, and offered me a hit. I politely declined. She took another deep drag, tilted her head back, and commented, "I've met Broderick, Albert, and Louisa, and I think I solved part of your haunting problems." She held out her glass for a refill. I dutifully filled her glass with Titos on the rocks and added a little OJ. She dramatically leaned back again, crossed her mile-long legs for effect, and continued, "The old man was a class 'A' asshole. He was stuck here because he made his wife dead and apparently arranged Albert's demise to get back the bucks he paid him for something he thought was stolen. Albert was hanging around because he didn't know who whacked him, how it was done, and why."

"You mean you *talked* to them?" I exclaimed. "All the two men have ever done around me or my guests is just show themselves."

"Yep" Lex answered. "And most of those sightings were just accidents. Nobody has anything to offer so they just hang around, kind of 'haunting' the place." She took a drink and smiled. "That is until I showed up. After the old man spilled his ghostly guts, I told Albert how he got bumped off and what the motive was. Apparently, there's some sort of afterlife council, and he ratted on Broderick, so they *un-haunted* the old man and sent him to where all the bad people go to toast for eternity. I guess it's okay with the ghost union to do bad stuff but you aren't supposed to keep it a secret amongst each other or something. That meant Albert got to cross over and rest forever. Two ghosts gone." She sat back in the lounge again, smiled her Cheshire cat smile, and triumphantly sipped her drink.

"That leaves Louisa," I ventured.

"Ah, Louisa," Lex answered. "Now that's a different kettle of fish. She's one tough, spoiled rotten Cuban biotch princess. You might be a little surprised, but she's not looking for the guy that did her in. She doesn't even think she's dead. She's here to guard over some huge gold cross. She says it's here but she won't say where."

"Here!" I jumped up, astonished. "It can't be here. I tore almost every wall in this building apart when we renovated and never found so much as a toe ring. Did she say where it is?"

"Nope," answered Lex. "Oh she knows where it's hidden, but also knows if it's found, it will most likely be locked up in a safety deposit box or some dusty museum, and she will have to follow it, and spend eternity in a place not of her choosing. I think she likes hanging around here. You're probably stuck with her forever. She ain't goin' nowhere."

"Can you ask her to stop crawling in the sack with me at night?" I asked. "It's kind of unnerving to wake up in the middle of the night with a ghost giving you a blowjob. I've taken to sleeping on my stomach. I must say though," I mused, "she is talented. That woman could suck the chrome off a trailer hitch."

"I will not," retorted Lex. "Every girl, even one living in the afterlife, wants a little nookie occasionally."

But I didn't "see" Louisa after that, at least not in my room. Lex must have called her off for a while.

The girls stuck around for a few weeks before checking out. They planned on taking U.S. One all the way north to Fort Kent Maine, then crossing the Canadian border and cruising part of Quebec before crossing back over the border someplace near Niagara Falls and heading back to the West coast. "Be careful when you cross the border," I warned. "That Porsche will light up the Mounties like a Christmas tree. I promise they will take it completely apart looking for contraband. Make sure you keep any prescription meds in their original bottles and leave any weed here, not to mention any Columbian marching powder."

"Never touch the stuff," retorted Lex. "It tickles my nose, and I forget what's going on. I usually wake up with a sore pussy." She paused, "Not that's an especially bad thing, but if I'm going to get pounded, I prefer to be awake to enjoy it. We can do without lighting up for a few weeks. I'll leave our pipes with you."

I got some nice hugs and a few more non-uncle-ish goodbye kisses and the Targa whirled away in a screech and a cloud of tire smoke.

A pessimist thinks all the girls in the world are bad and an optimist hopes to hell he's right. I don't think Lex will ever really grow up.

I hope she never does.

Flashback - August 1, 1715

The morning following the storm dawned clear, bright, and humid. Francisco, a seaman aboard the *San Miguel* was one of only a handful of crew from that ship to survive the storm. He lay at the water's edge and surveyed his surroundings. Ravenously thirsty, his prayers were answered when a brief shower passed over. Catching the rainfall in a piece of dirty canvas, he managed to quench his thirst. He waded among the mangroves throughout the day, gathering anything he thought might be of value. It was there he came upon one of the bodies, a Franciscan monk still wearing his familiar brown robes. He kneeled in the shallow water in prayer for the monk, whom he had known aboard the ship as Friar Accencio Rivera. He carefully rolled the body over and pulled the rings off the salt water-bloated fingers, probably breaking every digit in the process. He said a prayer of thanks and apology when he noticed a gold chain around the father's neck. Carefully, he pulled the chain over the father's neck and was surprised to see a large cross, encrusted with emeralds and a large red stone he couldn't identify. He first started to slip the cross around his neck, but realizing it would be immediately visible to any other survivors, he wrapped it in a scrap of the monk's robe and put it in his pocket.

Wet and hungry, the survivors of the *San Miguel* knew their only chance of survival was the beach and the chance a passing ship might rescue them. Clinging to pieces of shipwreck debris since none could swim; the remaining crew of the *San Miguel* made their way across the choppy waters of the Indian River Lagoon. After two days, and losing five more crewmates to exposure and one to a hungry bull shark, they reached Orchid Island on the Atlantic Shore, near the present-day Sebastian Inlet, although in 1715, there was thought to be no open passage from the sea at that time.

Much to their surprise, they found hundreds of shipmates from the other wrecks. Unlike the surviving crew of the *San Miguel,* there were several officers among the remaining members, and plans were quickly organized to send a party north by foot to the Spanish Fort of St. Augustine.

The beaches of Florida were littered with wreckage and bodies, and the survivors of this human tragedy were trying to comprehend what had happened to them. They were attempting to find their actual location. As the ships had wrecked at different locations, and were separated by sometimes several miles, it was impossible for the survivors to fully assess the extent of the disaster. They were stranded in this inhospitable land without food or water. Many were dying each day, adding to the already devastating number of casualties. Admiral Don Francisco Salmone undertook to immediately survey the extent of the damage. After observing that almost all ships had been wrecked, he decided, on August 6, to send a small crew to Cuba via launch to alert them to the tragedy, and to send a personal message to the governor, the Marques de Casatorres. It took ten days for the small boat to reach Havana.

The sailors survived for weeks on meager food and a little rainwater. The lagoon, thought to be mostly fresh before the inlet was cut, was brackish at the time due to the wash over from the hurricane and un-drinkable.

While awaiting rescue along with ship wreckage, tools, and a few meager provisions, no small amount of treasure, scattered amongst the wreckage, was amassed by the castaways, knowing fully well that the first "rescue" ship to arrive would take control of the piles of silver cobs, gold bars and a chest of gem quality emeralds that had been the personal possession of the Admiral. With no one person in charge, the crews anguished over what to do with the booty. "We should bury it," spoke up a first mate. "That way the ships that will soon be here cannot find the wealth." He took a handful of gold coins from the pile. "We have ship's tools in our possession that we have still not used for trade. Hammer these coins together into a large, flat sheet. We'll use it to make a map." Enthusiastically, the skip chandlers began pounding the pure gold coins out. Gold, especially in its purest form, can be pounded into very thin sheets.

Once done, they selected a spot with a recognizable landmark; an outcropping of limestone, shaped like a horse's head. Marking off fifty paces inland, they dug a deep hole and deposited the treasure. The next afternoon, an artisan carefully drew a precise map, showing the location of the hoard.

"What to do with the map?" asked the sailors. "If the ships come to plunder the wrecks, they will find this map as well. All of our work will be lost to them." The castaways anguished for days about how to hide the map without it being discovered. The answer came to them one night. In the moonlight, came a giant leatherback turtle, hoisting herself up the beach to lay her eggs. She was fully fifteen hundred pounds in weight. This queen of the sea was nearly as big as a modern-day compact car. The hungry sailors, starving for fresh meat, quickly descended upon the helpless turtle with knives and axes. "Wait," called a ship captain, "this is our answer. Legend has it these beasts return to the exact same beach where they were born every year. Let's attach the map to her shell before she returns to the sea. In the meantime, we can enjoy her eggs." The starving crew was much more in favor of butchering the reptile, knowing the huge supply of fresh turtle meat would last them for days. Noting the survivor's unrest, the captain, drew his pistol and leveled it at the crowd. Motioning to the ship's craftsmen he ordered. "You have the tools. Take some brass screws from the wreckage." Throwing the map on the sand he directed. "Here."

Reluctantly the ship's carpenters sat in the sand while the giant leatherback first dug a hole with her back flipper, then, crying sand-coated tears; she deposited over one hundred and ten soft eggs in the sand.

As soon as she finished, the sailors descended on the nest, scooping out the freshly hatched clutch, and passing the still-warm eggs out, hungrily sucked the contents out of each egg raw, while the captain watched carefully, pistol in hand to ensure the matriarch came to no harm.

Before the leatherback could return to the sea, the ship carpenters, positioned the hammered gold to the huge leathery back of the turtle, watching her safely lumber back to the sea, the captain un-cocked his pistol. "Now, next year, or years after, all any of us have to do is return to this place and the map to the wealth will come to you on the back of this beast."

Within a few days, several ships were leaving Havana harbor, loaded with emergency supplies, salvage equipment, government officials, and soldiers, making their way to the East Coast of Florida. Salvage was to begin as soon as the relief expedition reached the survivor's camps. Success came early as salvage sloops dragged the ocean floor for wreckage and quickly brought up chests of coins, as well as jewelry and gold. The Havana salvage *Flotta* was soon joined by ships sent from St. Augustine to help in the recovery effort. By early September, such was the success of the salvage team that Admiral Salmone wrote the governor asking him to send 25 soldiers and ammunition to guard the King's gold.

Tribes of local Indians, the *Ais* came upon the castaways after a few days. A smallish, diminutive tribe, they were nonetheless fierce and warlike and it became apparent that they planned on killing everyone. The soldiers among the survivors managed to hold off the Indians, and then some of the crew came forth with iron artifacts, knives, hatchets, and cutlasses, as gifts. The *Ais* not only calmed when the valuable iron items were offered, but they also brought the Spaniards wild game, fish, and vegetables. The crew hastily returned to the wrecks for more trade items. To the *Ais,* iron axes were worth far more than gold and silver coins.

The *Ais* Indians were native Floridians, and should not be confused with the Seminole Indians of a later date. Arriving in the Brevard area about 1000 AD, the *Ais* lived in small nomadic bands and chose various prime locations along the Indian River to make camp. The beach area was the normal winter habitat but with the coming of summer and the ever-present mosquitos, the Indians would migrate to the higher mainland ridges. They still came to the beach for clams and other seafood, and that's when they happened upon the survivors.

Physically, the *Ais* were small in stature in comparison with the average contemporary American Indian. Their small stature did not result in timidity, however, for all known accounts indicate that the *Ais* were proficient hunters and skilled in the use of the bow and arrow.

The main garb of the *Ais* men was a breechcloth, and many ornaments of stone, bone, and shell have been found throughout history which would indicate that the women's apparel was made of various animal skins. Hunting and fishing were the chief occupational opportunities and since wildlife was in abundance, food was no problem. Their staple food was fish speared from the Indian River which was known to the *Ais* Tribe as the "Aysta-chatta-hatch-ee." Translated, this means "the river of the Ais Indians." Later the Spaniards were to refer to the Indian River on all of their maps as "The Rio d'Ays." In addition to fish and game, oysters, clams, and snails were a mainstay of their diet land this is what they shared with the shipwrecked sailors.

By the time the weather and sea conditions had become unsuitable for continuing salvage, in late October of the same year, over five million silver pieces of eight had been recovered along with numerous gold coins and bars, jewelry, and a great part of the King's treasure. Although salvage was essentially completed, efforts continued well into 1718.

News of the disaster had swept the Americas and Europe and privateers, pirates and looters converged toward Palmar de Ayes (near present-day Sebastian, Florida) like ravenous vultures. Early in January 1716, pirate Henry Jennings aboard his well-armed sloop, the 40-ton *Barsheba*, and John Wills aboard his 35-ton *Eagle*, both having been commissioned by Governor Hamilton of Jamaica, attacked the Spanish salvage camp at Palmar de Ays, and detained the defenders. While looting the camp, they made off with some 120,000 pieces of eight and other valuables, as well as two bronze cannon and two large iron guns.

In total, eleven ships were lost, sunk offshore, washed up on the beach, or in the case of the *San Miguel*, washed completely over the beachfront and up the shallow Indian River Lagoon. The wreck finally sunk in shallow water.

There it lay, undiscovered for three hundred years.

8
No Shortage of Genuine Treasure Maps in this Town

On most Mondays, I let Matilda, Bela, Marcus, and Scarlet take the day off. Usually, we had no guests so all I have to worry about for breakfast is me. I buttered some toast and sat down poolside for a quiet meal when Cousin Eddie gave one of his quiet 'you have company' woofs. Going to the door, I saw a guy in his mid-50s, wearing a dirty torn tee shirt, shorts, well-worn Sperry Topsiders, and a baseball cap. His nose and cheeks were sunburned.

"Come back later this week to paint the fence!" I yelled through the door.

"I need a room" came the voice from the other side. "I was told by a friend of a friend of a friend that you might be interested in this as trade." He held out a necklace toward the screen with a coin hanging on it. I peered through the door and could see the unmistakable shine of gold.

"I blew my last thirty dollars on gas to get here and I don't have enough gas left to get ten miles back up the road." I opened the door a crack and could see it was a gold doubloon. From its looks, I would guess it was probably from the seventeen hundreds. "What will this get me?" He asked in a meek voice.

"Maybe two weeks if it's real," I answered, opening the door a crack more.

"Oh, I assure you, my friend it's very real. Make it three weeks, and it's a deal." I hesitated for a moment and figured, what the Hell. It's off-season and that coin might bring fifteen grand, depending on its age, and if it's really genuine. Anyway, he looked like he had a good story or two in him and I was bored with nothing better to do.

"Deal," I answered. He slipped the necklace over his head and handed it through the door. I absently dropped it in my shirt pocket without examining it any further. If it was a fake, even a good fake I would be able to tell the difference. It did feel heavy enough that I was sure at least the gold bezel was eighteen carats.

"I've worn that for over ten years," he remarked. "It will feel strange without it, I guess I'll need to go find another." He stuck out his hand. "Matt Black," he introduced himself. "Russell Phillips." I almost automatically answered, allowing him in. I sat down at the front desk and fished the necklace out of my pocket for a more thorough examination. A genuine gold doubloon or a damn good reproduction. I couldn't see a date anywhere but that's no surprise. By its design and the inscription REX PHILIPUS V. DG. HISPANIRUM (King Philip V by the Grace of God King of Spain) I would guess early eighteenth century. "Where did you find that?" I asked. He chuckled quietly. "What's so funny?" I asked. "Any place but the keys or around Sebastian where I come from, you would have said, 'Where did you buy that?' In this neck of the woods, you ask 'Where did you find that? Yes, I found it myself, someplace a little north, and if you're wondering, there's probably more where it came from."

I fixed him a cup of coffee, pouring in a healthy portion of Makers Mark, first into his cup, and then mine, and invited him poolside to chat. I started, "What brings you to the rock?"

"Everybody needs a little time away," he answered cryptically. "And I needed to get away for a while."

"Yeah, that and the next three lines to the Christopher Cross song," I replied. "Well, this is as a good a place as any to hide, even when no one's chasing." I paused, but he didn't rise to the bait.

He sipped his spiked coffee and left for his room, not offering any more conversation, so I let him be. He looked like he hadn't slept for a week, so I guessed an early bedtime was in his plan. I didn't see him till breakfast the next morning.

He hung around for a few weeks, eating my breakfast like a horse, like it was his only meal of the day, (which it probably was). He left every morning after breakfast and came back every afternoon looking tired and dejected, dragging his ass, as we used to say in the

Navy. I figured if he wanted to talk, eventually he would eventually open up.

Or not.

So one night, about two weeks into his stay, Matt joined me for happy hour, as he did every night since the first night. Like breakfast, which he dove into every morning like a starving man, he wasted no time getting outside of a generous supply of my good liquor. I tried to start his motor one more time.

"You look like a man with a sad story," I ventured.

"I've had better months." Was all he ventured, looking up at the trees.

He took another long pull from his drink. I guess the whiskey loosened him up a little.

After a minute's silence he spoke, "I chose Key West for a reason," he started. "You see, I'm a treasure diver."

"No shortage of those down here," I ventured, cautiously.

"Exactly," he responded. "But I'm on to something big, and I don't have the resources to exploit it. I thought maybe if I came down here, I could find an investor. But it appears I'm not the only person with a treasure map and a golden mission." He looked up at me, holding his glass out for another refill. I topped him off and refreshed my own vodka/cran while I was at it.

Matt looked left and right in an exaggerated fashion as if to see we were alone. He started his story in the middle as if I already knew the beginning.

"There were a dozen ships in the 1715 Plate fleet that sunk off the east coast of Florida. All but one was lost in a hurricane. But of the eleven that were lost, only seven wrecks have ever been found and salvaged." He leaned a little closer. "Thirty years ago, some so-called treasure hunters rediscovered those seven wrecks, and probably all the anchors and cannons for most of the others. They made easy money from the large artifacts selling them to restaurants, souvenir stands, shell shops, and gas stations from Miami to Jacksonville. They didn't have anything like GPS and didn't even mark where they found the stuff on a chart, and now since they pulled up all the big stuff, and more importantly, so much of the ferrous metal that they can't find the rest of the ships.

Lots of people searched everywhere but never found the missing ships. At least for one of the wrecks, I'm pretty sure they were searching in the wrong place."

"So you found one? Where?"

"That's for me to know and you to find out," he answered. I don't know if the Jamesons was talking or he was being a smartass.

I took one last pull on my drink, sat it on the table, and stood up. "Mr. Black, if that's your real name, I don't have time to play games. If you want some help, I might be able to put you in front of the right people, but I need a little more proof before I invest people's time and money in some harebrained scheme."

He stood up too "Calm down, Mr. Phillips," he said. "I've lost everything I own by trusting the wrong people. I have to be careful. Everyone looks for the wrecks just off the Atlantic coast, but not inland on the Sebastian River. You see that inlet didn't exist in 1715, but with a big enough storm surge and a high tide a ship might have been pushed over the beach and right into the Indian River."

I took the conversation in a different direction. I needed more information. "You say you lost everything, which means you at least once had something," I said.

"Oh yeah, lots of dive gear and a boat," he answered. "Not a great boat, but a decent boat."

"Did you use a mailbox or airlift?" I queried, referring to the large curved tubes used to divert prop wash downward to clear loose debris off the seafloor.

Me and my big mouth.

The answer was almost absently automatic. "Can't use either," he answered. "Too shallow. Almost on land." He suddenly stopped and looked at me. "Hey, how do you know about mailboxes?"

I looked sheepish when I answered. "Oh, I've read about them someplace."

He looked straight into my eyes, "Don't try to bullshit a bullshitter," he muttered. "You've worked wrecks."

I just sat there, sipping my drink, and kept my mouth shut. I had said enough.

Black stared at me for a few minutes and then stood up. "Wait here," he blurted. "I have something to show you." And he headed up the back stairs to his room. I couldn't help but see a diaphanous image in a green flowing gown follow him up the stairs. He returned a moment later with a binder and charts under his arm. Sweeping away an ashtray and some wet cocktail napkins, he spread a chart on the glass-top patio table. With the map open, he pointed to an area I was slightly familiar with. "I'm going to show you something I've never shown anyone else. Not even my so-called 'partner'. This is a chart from about 1880 before there was even an inlet dug at Sebastian. You can clearly see the area where the inlet was eventually cut and all the islands around the Indian River."

"Hell, I was there several years ago, ah, doing work for some people," I answered. (Diving on the 1715 fleet). "I would go fishing in the Indian River on my days off. You can hardly call them islands." I remarked. "They are nothing more than glorified sandbars. Maybe a few pines, occasionally a sea grape, and a few bushes. Not much more."

"Exactly!" Matt exclaimed. "Now, look at this chart from 1936. The U.S. and the state government, along with some local businessmen tried to open the inlet almost constantly from the late 1880s till the 1920's, but it kept filling back in almost instantly with sand and mud from the river flow to the sea. They finally got it open in 1923, and it's been open ever since except for a period during World War Two, when they let it close up on purpose for security reasons, to keep U-boats out of the Indian River. Before that, the Indian River was more like a stagnant freshwater pond."

"What's that got to do with the price of tea in China?" I asked, sarcastically.

Matt grinned. "Look closer, at the named islands. Now look at the old chart. What's missing?"

I peered at the charts closely. "Smigel Island isn't showing on the old chart?" I ventured, slowly.

"You got it!" he shouted. "Like you said, it's hardly more than a sandbar. It wasn't there before the Sebastian inlet was opened and water started flowing in and out. It's not an island, it's a wreck. It lay just a few feet underwater, and when the inlet started flowing, the wreckage started catching sand and it made a little island. I bet there's a chart from before this 1880 map, probably in Spanish showing a wreck site. Whoever made this 1936 chart had a copy of that map, and misunderstood the wreck location for the *San Miguel*, which would have been noted as S Miguel, and named that sand bar Smigel Island. Another name bastardized by lazy Americans like Cayo Hueso, Bone Island, became Key West, and lost to history."

"So you're looking for a partner," I asked, changing the subject again. If I pour enough vodka in me, my attention span goes to shit, my dick won't get hard at the most inopportune time, and my vision blurs.

Black looked cautious. "I had a 'partner' he said slowly. That's why I only have the shirt on my back and that busted-down pickup truck. I don't have any salvage equipment, dive gear, a boat, a pot to piss in, or a window to throw it out of. I don't want a partner. I'm looking for an investor."

I sat back down with a heavy sigh. "I understand, Mr. Black," I answered. "I've been burned a few times myself trusting the wrong people. People have even died because of that trust. I assure you I'm honest and can be trusted. (Except for some gold bars, I found once under a cannon, I remembered.)" I pondered for a second and came to a decision. "This is in complete confidence. You guessed right about me being a diver. I'm here myself under the Witness Protection Program. I'm a professional salvage diver, or at least I used to be. I was up in Sebastian twenty years ago working on the 1715 fleet, and I actually found a little wreck sometime back just west of Key West. I know how hard it is trying to find a loaded treasure ship. You have to look under thousands of square miles for a spot about the size of a house, and you can go right past a wreck forty feet underwater and never recognize it.

There's a better chance of finding silver than gold, and for that matter, there's a better chance of finding the money pit on Oak Island or having an E.T. walk into city hall tomorrow and file for citizenship. It seems like you're putting a lot of effort into the chance of finding a little silver." I reached back into my memory banks. "The *Santísima Trinidad,* also called the *Urca de Lima* was found on the Indian River years ago. Everybody and their brother dived on that wreck and found nothing. The salvage crews three hundred years ago picked her clean. And for that matter, back in the day, you could walk halfway to Nassau and never get your feet wet by stepping from treasure boat to treasure boat. I got to believe that whole coast has been picked over."

"I'm not talking about not the *Urca,*" he countered. "That's old news. Like I said, I think this was the *San Miguel,* and she had treasure in her. Lots. And as for being picked over, they are still pulling millions off the Treasure Coast. Based on the ship's manifests, there's probably over half a billion dollars worth of gold, silver, and emeralds still undiscovered out there on the east coast of Florida, more than they pulled off the *Atocha and the Santa Maria* down here."

He leaned forward in his chair again, taking another sip of his drink. "It's not a 'little silver' I'm looking for, How about a priceless gold cross, weighing more than half a pound?"

That stopped me in my tracks. "What kind of cross?" I asked

"A big gold one, crusted with emeralds and rubies," he answered. "Made for the Queen of Spain, a long time ago and lost in the hurricane. It was on the ship's manifest that it was somewhere aboard the *San Miguel.*"

"Describe it a little more," I asked, carefully. That cross sounded very familiar.

"It's this big!" He repeated, holding his hands about six inches apart. "According to the archives in Seville, Spain, it was somewhere aboard that ship, but it doesn't say where. Probably in the safekeeping of some trusted individual, like a nobleman or a member of the clergy. There aren't any drawings or paintings, but I can show you this. It was drawn from first-hand accounts of the design, taken in Peru in 1713. I had a friend hand draw this off the original drawing in the archives in Seville, Spain." He opened the binder and unfolded a wrinkled, well-worn piece of paper, handing it to me.

I took it and spread it on the table under the light. It was a crude drawing of a cross with stones on all four corners and a stone in the middle. The corners were marked "esmeralda" (emerald) and the central stone had an arrow that said "rubi" (ruby), all in Spanish.

I hated to burst his bubble but I had to show him. "Come with me. I want you to see something." I stood up again and opened the back door to the house. Puzzled, Matt followed me inside and down the hall. Out of habit, I held the door for Louisa, out of politeness, as she chose for some reason, to tag along, even though she was quite capable of floating through walls. I don't think she was making herself known to Matt. If he could see her, he wasn't saying anything. The three of us stopped in front of a familiar painting. "I don't think you will find that cross, at least not under the ocean."

He was dumbfounded as he stared at the painting of Louisa with the exact same cross as the drawing described. "Well, I'll be dipped in shit," he remarked. "How the hell did that cross get to Key West?"

I motioned to Matt to return to the patio. He sat in a chair and put his head in his hands, "I've spent the last twenty years chasing this thing, and now I learn it isn't even near where I thought it was. I give up."

"Matt, it's not all a lost cause," I answered. "I believe if your theory is right, you pretty well know where the *San Miguel* lay. Surely it was carrying more treasure than one gold cross."

"You're right, according to the manifest, it had several million dollars' worth of silver coins, bullion gold doubloons, and emeralds, plus loads of fine china, and there's nothing in the archives that says any of it was recovered by the Spanish," he went on. "Not to mention all the undocumented treasure it almost certainly had on board. It's a rich wreck."

"Do you think it's still there?" I asked.

"I don't believe the *San Miguel* was ever exploited by the salvage crews, both right after the fleet sunk, and was never worked by Kip Wagner or his hired gun young Mel Fisher back in the sixties. I think everything's still there. I wouldn't have figured out the location, but some grandma hooked an old deadeye with her anchor one day when she was fishing in the bay. They brought a barge with a crane on it to the site and pulled it up plus some timbers, a six-pound gun, and an anchor. It got me thinking and looking at charts, and there it was, clear as the nose on my face. Her story made the local papers but no place else. I paid her a grand to show me where she found the stuff, and another grand to not tell anyone else. She contracted Alzheimer's a few years later. She constantly talks about the wreck, but she also insists she can show you where the Martians landed, and where the Skunk Ape lives. She can tell you who was the vice presidential candidate for the losing party in the 1948 election, but she doesn't remember what she had for breakfast this morning. I don't think anyone believes any of her stories. I knew her before she crossed that rainbow bridge. I *know* that story is true."

He then gave me a few more clues to convince me. "That's where I found that coin you have," he continued. "I picked it right off the sandbar on Smigel Island one day after a storm. Where there's one, there has to be more."

"So you are telling me you are the only person on the planet who knows the location of a bunch of gold, a pile of silver bars and God knows what else," I concluded. "Forget the cross. Go back to the Indian River, find the wreck, file a salvage claim, and get rich."

"I wish it was that easy," he said quietly. "That wreck sits in a nature preserve. You pick up anything bigger than a pelican turd inside that preserve, and if it's fifty years old or older, the Guvmit will toss you in jail and throw away the key."

I thought for a minute. "You need to be sneaky and pretend you're fishing. My buddy has a brother up that way with a nice boat. It's a Conch33 fishing boat. I'm sure Blotto would be happy to lease it to you by the week. I can make some calls in the morning."

"Blotto?" Matt asked. "What kind of name is Blotto?"

"It comes from his high school days," I answered. "He didn't know when he was one beer or three over the limit, and he drank himself blotto every Saturday night."

"Ah, got it," replied Black. "Hopefully he got over that habit."

"He has," I answered. "Nowadays he just smokes himself blind every night with Cannabis."

He looked at me quizzically, not sure if I was joking or not. I just kept my mouth shut.

Changing the subject, I said, "Let me check into it. I'll front you some cash to get you going. Once you are sure of the wreck location, let me know. It's in shallow water, almost on land, and being away from any big wave action, I will hazard a guess there's not too much overburden. Find the main pile, harvest as much as you can, take it three miles out into the Atlantic and 'find' it again. Voila!"

I went on, a little more animated. The treasure hunter in me was waking up.

"Berth the boat in Fort Pierce, if you can. It's a longer commute every day, but it won't draw as much attention as it would someplace nearer." I reached into my desk and pulled out my Glock nine-millimeter. "Here, it's a little protection if you get in a tight spot." I hesitated for a second. "Get a few buddies and they can pretend to be fishing while you work a metal detector. The baddies won't recognize the boat and just think it's a tourist fishing for snook."

He thought about the scenario I created for a minute. "That might just work," answered Black slowly. He suddenly looked into my eyes.

"What's in it for you?"

I had that part figured out already. "Strictly business. After being reimbursed for all my expenses, I get ten percent of your net. Paid in cash, not treasure. My handshake's a contract. More binding to me than a document."

"Deal," Matt answered, sticking out his hand after a moment's hesitation. "And if we don't score?"

"Then we'll write it all off to adventure," I answered. "But something tells me it's gonna score and big."

We exchanged phone numbers and he gathered up his few belongings. I called Rumpy and asked him to reach out to certain people. After that, I went upstairs to my private stash for some starter loot to give to Matt for a grubstake.

The next morning I met Matt in the lobby, me with an envelope with some cash and him with a binder, two charts, and a toothbrush.

We shook hands and before he turned to leave I spoke. "Wait a moment." Reaching into my pocket, I pressed the gold-bezeled *Escudo* into his palm. "Here," I said. "I think this means more to you than me." He slowly took the coin and placed it back around his neck. We shook hands again. "I…"

There was a tear in his right eye, "Oh shut the fuck up," I said. "Or we'll both start bawling like babies. Now get out of here before I change my mind, and keep that coin so you will return and buy it back from me."

Without another word, he turned and walked toward his truck.

I didn't know that was the last time we would ever meet.

Later that day, feeling lonely, I finally got word to my kids via the people who assisted with my identity change. They would be happy that the news of my unfortunate demise was greatly exaggerated. I did stress it would be best to stay away, just in case all the people I pissed off were still watching for them. It was unlikely, but it was better to be safe than sorry. Since my old somewhat buddy Tim Hemminger was retired and living in Baja, I arranged it through some of his former work chums who monitored my participation in the witness protection program. They were none too happy that I had put down roots back in Key West but I knew living any place else would kill me as quick as any bullet. Grace Alice was obviously happy daddy-o was still alive and kicking and agreed to stay far away at college in Washington, as long as I paid an occasional visit.

Brody, on the other hand, was standing on my doorstep, the following night.

"You are piss-poor at following directions," I growled.

"I had a good teacher," replied Brody. "Besides, I've been aboard a treasure dive ship off the Carolina coast for months on the trail of a real pirate ship. There's no way anyone would have been watching me." I had to agree with his logic but sequestered him in my private room, warning him not to speak to anyone, save Scarlet, who knew each other well. He grudgingly agreed, and moved into my man cave, dumping my vodka stash out of the freezer onto the floor, he loaded the fridge with a few cases of root beer. He finished converting my room by hooking up the TV with his Game Boy. I saw him once a day at breakfast. He never came down for my happy hour and he had pizza delivered every night. Either Scarlet or I met the delivery guy at the door and delivered it upstairs. I always felt like I was lowering a cow into the raptor pen in Jurassic Park. I would hand over the pizza, and five minutes later an empty box would come sailing out the window. But I didn't really mind; it was good to have him around, and I was happy he was staying out of sight.

Flashback - August 1715

For the next few years, the Spanish rescue ships maintained their shore side camp while they worked at recovering what they could of the lost treasure. Meanwhile, all who were not needed for this tremendous task were sent back to Havana or on to St. Augustine. The logistics of maintaining and feeding such a large number of people on that isolated sandy shore was difficult. There were also the disciplinary problems of keeping order among these stranded adventurers and dealing with their attempts to conceal portions of the recovered treasure for themselves.

The authorities in St. Augustine also had to be dealt with. Florida was probably Spain's poorest province in the New World, and it was considered an unpopular duty to be stationed there. With such wealth lying at their very doorstep, naturally, they expected a share of it to be channeled through their own settlement. To their dismay, orders were received that all that was recovered was to be returned to Havana for reshipment to Spain. The work of underwater salvage must have been difficult for there was little equipment available for the purpose.

The salvagers soon found that most of the ships were in such shallow water close to shore that much of the time they were hampered by heavy wave surges, breaking seas, and low underwater visibility. If the vessels had gone down further off shore in deeper water, the only way of reaching the cargo was by diving without air or by utilizing a crude diving bell which provided an airspace underwater into which the diver could stick his head now and then and gulp a breath of air. Few of the Spaniards had any experience in handling themselves under water. They relied chiefly upon the skill of Indian divers who were brought in to do their diving for them. The salvage crew worked chiefly upon the *Capitana* and *Almiranta* which lay near the shore in fairly shallow water. These ships also carried the bulk of the treasure.

By August 1716, the first shipment of the recovered wealth had arrived safely in Cadiz. In all, the salvors succeeded in recovering for the crown about four million pesos. It was observed, because of the sudden increment of currency circulation that the corsairs did not care whether the public treasury benefited or not. Surprisingly, it had not taken long for news of the shipwreck to travel to all the ports of that remote part of the world.

Soon after the first rescue ships arrived from Havana, even while the Spaniards were diving upon the stranded vessels, small sailing craft appeared from nowhere to dive upon the outlying wrecks to salvage whatever they could reach. The Spaniards, however after a few unsuccessful forays, gave up trying to drive off these petty pilferers. They were too busy with the aid of the Indian divers recovering and storing the wealth of the galleons they were working on.

There was little difference between pirate and privateer in those days when England, Spain, and France were in almost constant conflict. By 1716, the war of the Spanish Succession had been over more than three years, yet the pirate Henry Jennings, who had carried a patent from Jamaica to act as a privateer during the war, still terrorized the seas from Jamaica, his former headquarters, to the northernmost part of the Bahamas from his base at the pirate stronghold of New Providence.

Waiting until the Spaniards had labored for months to accumulate a storehouse full of the sunken treasure, Jennings gathered together a small fleet of two brigs and three long ships along with three hundred men. He set out to attack the Spanish settlement and secure the treasure. His informers had already told him that the hoard was guarded by two commissaries and a detachment of about sixty soldiers. Most of the encampment would be dispersed at the various diving locations. So it was not difficult to surprise the Spanish, kill or scare away the guardians of the storehouse, and make off with the 340,000 pesos it contained.

A series of small raids and the increasing difficulty of reaching the remaining treasure now locked in inaccessible parts of the lost ships which were rapidly breaking up in the succession of storms that followed year after year finally brought an end to the official recovery efforts. No doubt for many years thereafter, the bones of whatever wrecks could be reached would continue to be picked from hundreds of small craft. After the eastern shore of Florida became more settled late in the following century, it became commonplace for miles along the beaches to pick up coins and other small objects from the sunken treasure fleet which had by that time disappeared completely beneath the surface of the sea.

The finders had little idea from whence they came. For, on the shore where the Spanish camp had stood, the storehouse that protected the treasure and the crude barracks and other shelters had gradually fallen apart and disappeared beneath the ever-encroaching sand and jungle growth. Even the wells that had been sunk and lined with wooden hogsheads joined with pitch vanished beneath the accumulation of detritus.

The sailor Francisco, however, never took part in that recovery. With the gold cross carefully hidden under his ragged dirty shirt, he rode the first salvage galleon to return to Havana in 1715. Francisco arrived in Havana Harbor after two week's voyage aboard the salvage ship. No free passage, he worked every day as a seaman, furling the sails and maintaining the rigging, and received two bits, one-fourth of a Spanish Eight Real, a week for his effort. Paid in cash at the end of the trip, he walked down the gangplank on to Havana docks, promising the first mate he would be back in a few days. He actually had no intention of returning to the ship, although the ship's first mate had no idea.

In early eighteenth-century Cuba, the chief industry was stock-raising, an effort that was followed on all parts of the island. The meat was shipped live to various places and the hides were also exported, along with rendered beef fat or tallow, a critical commodity for the making of candles and soap. The sugar cane industry grew slowly and three sugar mills were established in its vicinity as early as the 1500s. These mills were simple, crude constructions of rollers for crushing the cane to extract the syrup for making rum, operated by cattle or water power. The product was obtained by simply boiling in open pans and was of a very inferior quality and it was consumed on the island.

Francisco's primary goal was to find a buyer for the cross before someone discovered it and took it away. He decided to start with a local merchandise store. He entered the nearest one. Surrounded by smelly hides, barrels of tallow, along with plates and cloth from China, he was immediately approached by the proprietor, ready to throw out a low-life commoner with no shoes, a dirty shirt, and torn trousers in tatters below the knee. Hat in hand, Francisco stood his ground. "Senor, I am a seaman, and I'm tired of the sea. I wish to work on a farm. Can you direct me toward the nearest plantation?"

The store owner stopped in his tracks, arrogant and oppressive, and glared at Francisco.

"There is a small sugar plantation just outside of town, belonging to Don Imhuilo Galarza" the proprietor slowly answered. "I suppose you could inquire with him. Now, leave, you filthy swine! You stink and you're defiling my store!"

Fernando looked at his surroundings and could hardly think his unwashed body could smell worse, but he hastily retreated from the mercantile and walked in the direction the store owner pointed. Nearing the outskirts of town, he stopped to bathe in a pond, clothes and all, the first time he had bathed in over a year. Asking further directions from a peasant in an oxcart, he finally found the farm. Far from looking like a plantation, he found a slovenly shack with a few acres of sugar cane under cultivation and a dozen slaves drudging under the hot sun with surly Imhuilo Galarza watching over them, a worn musket in hand. He swung his attention and the musket toward Francisco when he saw him walk up the dusty path. Galarza looked hardly like the Don title that the mercantile owner had called him.

"What do you want?" Galarza asked, gun still pointing at him.

"I have something to sell," stammered Fernando. "You may not be interested."

"You mean I may not be able to afford it," replied the owner. "Show me what you have."

Fernando hesitated, and then slowly reached into his pocket. Wrapped in dirty cloth, he handed the cross to Galarza.

Opening the cloth, he was astounded at the jewel-encrusted gold cross, with five huge emeralds and one ruby. "Where did this come from?" he asked.

"I found it. Far from here"

Galarza looked at the seaman shrewdly. "Who else knows about this?" he asked

"Nobody, I just landed this morning, from *La Florida,"* he

withheld the rest of the story.

Fernando didn't expect Galarza's response as the musket, still pointing at his chest, exploded from only five feet away, killing him instantly.

"Santos!" the owner cried out. "Come here! I caught this man trying to steal from me! Go quickly into town and tell the Alcalde to send troops!"

Imhuilo Galarza returned to his adobe hut. First making sure no one was near; he carefully pulled out a loose adobe brick and extracted a small wooden chest. Opening it, he placed his new treasure atop a meager pile of gold and silver coins. "Always look like a poor farmer," he mused to himself. He had saved every cob and escudo he'd collected over the years, amassed in the growing lucrative sugar cane plantation, living in the image of poverty in the process, He placed the chest back in the wall, carefully replaced the mud brick and went back to his slaves.

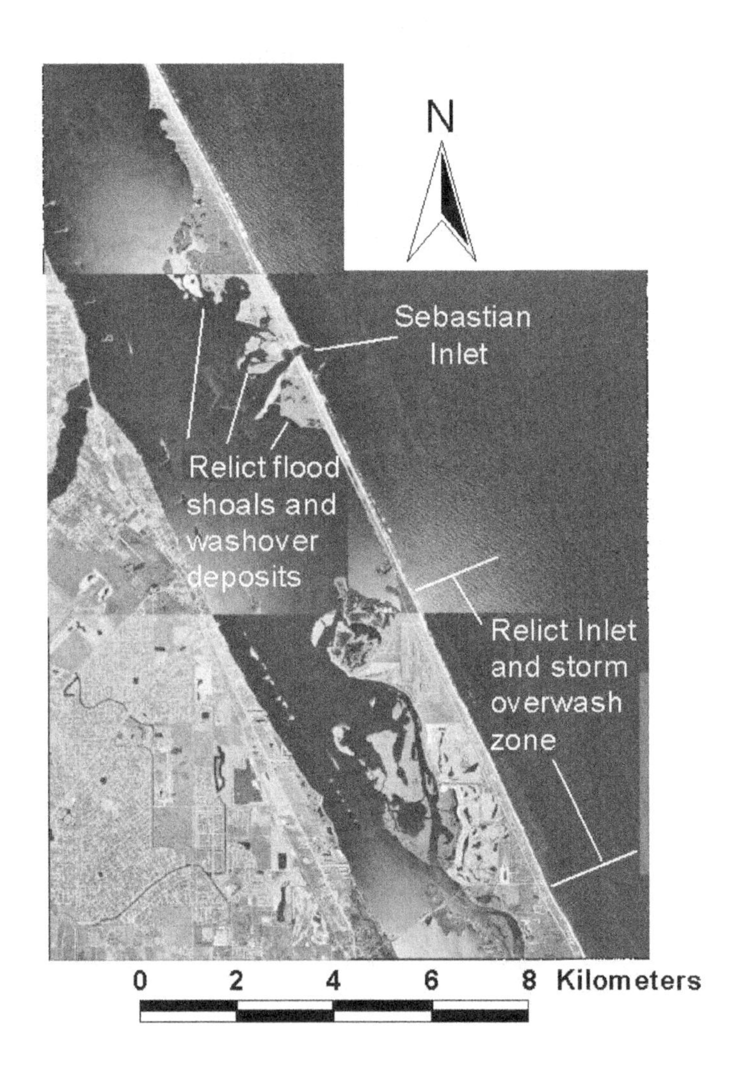
N
Sebastian
Inlet
Relict flood
shoals and
washover
deposits
Relict Inlet
and storm
overwash
zone
0
2
4
6
8
Kilometers

9
Right Coast, Wrong Columbus

It was another "me" Monday with everybody else off, about a month after Matt Black's visit. I was puttering in the kitchen early in the morning when a truck pulled up. It appeared to be a rust-bucket older Chevy Crew Cab. Two guys got out. Swarthy, mean-looking dudes to say the least. One stood outside and the other came in. Cousin Eddie, normally lying comatose on the porch under his favorite sunbeam, was watching this guy with rapt attention, a low growl rumbling from his throat. "You Mister Russell, the manager?" he asked

I stepped up to the front desk with my apron still on. "It depends on who wants to know," I answered, motioning to Eddie with one hand to cool it.

"You had a visitor about a month ago," he answered. "You gave him some info. Please tell me what you told him."

He leaned forward with his hands on the table. A gold chain with a coin on it swung forward. I couldn't help but recognize that coin and bezel hanging at the end. I had handed it back to Matt Black the day he left.

"I don't have any idea what you're talking about," I lied. "I'm not even sure who you're talking about. We get lots of visitors, but if it was a guy wearing a gold coin, like that." I poked him in the chest, looking into his eyes with a knowing stare, "he stayed here for a few weeks and left. I don't know where he was headed. We didn't talk much."

"I think you do know. Now please be polite and share."

"Look," I repeated. "We get lots of guests. That's why we're called a 'guest' house. I make it my business not to ask them about their business." (*Except good looking milfy-ish females*).

"You're wasting my time," he threatened. "Tell me what you know, and I'm out of your life."

My reaction was to reach for the phone. He held up one hand. "You don't want to call the cops," he said. "Bad idea."

"Oh, I'm not calling the cops," I answered, casually. "I'm calling an ambulance. They need to come to pick up two low lifers with multiple contusions, facial disfigurements, and numerous broken bones."

The thug reached for the phone and slammed it back on the receiver. I was about to start rearranging his nose when he reached into his jacket and pulled out a stainless steel Smith and Wesson with a two-inch barrel. With a barrel big enough to put my finger into, I would guess a forty-four. Eddie came right to his feet at the sight of the gun. I motioned him to lie down again. He grudgingly complied, but still kept rapt attention on the action.

"Time for playing games is over," he said, with a threatening voice. "I was hoping you would just tell me where the cross was, but we're gonna have to do it the hard way."

"Cross?" I answered, with an exaggerated voice, and the best fake grin I could conjure up. "Oh, why didn't you tell me?" I said. "He didn't come here asking about the cross. He already thought he knew where it was." I pointed toward the parlor. "I explained to him, I even showed him proof. That cross wasn't where he thought it was."

"I don't believe you," he said. "So you're gonna keep its location from me too?" Without giving me a chance to show, or explain, he motioned with the gun. "Get up. We're taking a ride." Pointing the gun at the dog, he cocked the six-shooter and threatened. "Do it or the first bullet goes to your mutt."

Eddie had never seen a gun in his life but sensed the danger. I could see the fur on the back of his neck rise, his body tense, and his lips begin to curl up. A low growl started again, deep in his throat. He wasn't 'my' dog. He hardly ever paid attention to me, came when I called only if it suited him, and didn't ever rely on me for most of his food, but it was apparent he was ready and willing to give his life for mine.

This shit was about to get real.

"Ed," I said sternly. I didn't know if he would mind, but I had to try. His ears went back; he yawned nervously and looked at me with a worried expression, then whined quietly and laid down again.

I stalled, idly doodling for a moment on an open chart that was on the desk. After a few moments, I put my pen down and stood up. It's hard to argue much when a loaded pistol is pointed at your chest. Oh, I suppose I could have figured out a way to end it there, but it would have resulted in a lot of undesirable investigations by the local authorities and the good chance someone would have figured out who I *really* was. If I just disabled them and called the cops, they might have been in trouble for waving a gun, but no crime had been committed.

Yet. Best I take this situation off the rock.

I stalled a little more. "Let me lock up the inn and call someone to come in to cover. Nobody else is here yet." (And wouldn't be all day.) I didn't mention that Brody was fast asleep upstairs in my room. "If I just vanish, somebody will notify to police."

"Let 'em" he answered. "By the time they notice you are missing, nobody will have a clue where you have gone."

I could have made this a short visit, but I was curious what they had in mind. Besides, with a cannon like that casually pointing at me, I didn't want any accidents accidently happening to me.

At gunpoint, I walked to the crew cab; hoping one of my neighbors would notice the commotion. Just my luck that the crazy lady living next door with two poodles and six cats that snooped at everything I did so she could gossip to the neighbors, was nowhere in sight. Sitting in the back, his buddy took the gun and kept it trained on me. Eddie stood at the door, whining in helplessness.

"Shouldn't we tie him up or something, Greg?" Asked the accomplice.

"Nah, Ollie, he talks like he's a badass but he's just an old cook." Answered the guy that answered to Greg. "I'm sure he's harmless."

I just smiled a thin smile, put my head back on the headrest, and took a nap.

We drove in silence for a while. "Where are we going?" I asked after an hour or so. I figured nothing ventured, nothing gained. "We're gonna see if being in the area, plus a little 'extra' persuading, might jog your memory."

We got to our destination, someplace on U.S. 1, about five or six hours north of Key West sometime toward dark. I didn't know where I was until I saw a sign that said Micco. They pulled around back of a dilapidated singlewide and into a fenced yard. To anyone else, it would appear abandoned, but to these guys, it was a pure mansion. "Get out, and walk slowly toward the door," ordered Greg. "And don't try anything funny. This trailerhood ain't afraid of, or unaccustomed to a few pistol shots in the night." I went to the door. Keys were produced and I was roughly shoved inside. If you thought the outside was a bit rustic, it didn't hold a candle to the interior. Clothes, bedding, and garbage were piled to the ceiling everywhere. You could tell the last meal that was cooked was shrimp and nobody bothered to empty the trash.

I was hungry, having not eaten breakfast since the morning before. There was a bottle of Code Rum sitting on the table. Boy, a swig about now would really taste heavenly.

After walking into that heap at least my appetite was gone.

"Sit down!" Ordered Ollie, pistol in hand. I complied, sitting in the only chair not covered in garbage, a plastic outdoor chair like you find for five bucks at a Walmart. He grabbed a rope that was lying on the floor. It smelled like it had last been used to tie up a dead yak. "I'm gonna make sure you stick around tonight."

"With digs this nice, I wouldn't dream of leaving," I quipped. That earned me a blow across the back of the head with something wet and heavy. I shudder to think what it was. With the gun pointed at me, I decided to let him live for a while longer. With Greg holding me at gunpoint, Ollie hogtied me, hand and foot, then roughly pushed me off the chair into the pile of rubbish. They turned out the light and went into the living room, closing the door.

I stayed like that for two days, only getting relief for potty breaks and an occasional drink of foul-tasting warm tap water. They didn't grace me with the reason for hanging around, but I overheard then remarking that it was too rough to get on the water, even the Intracoastal.

On the third morning, before sunrise, I was roughly kicked awake. "Wake up!" Greg said. "We're goin' for a little boat ride."

"Look," I explained. "I told you before, that the cross, if there is one, isn't located on a wreck. If you had been a little less hasty, I could have proved it to you. As for the wreck, I'll tell you everything I know. It's supposed to be in the Indian River, about three hundred yards below someplace called Smigel Island." I gave him a location exactly three hundred yards on the other side of the island from where Matt told me he thought the wreck really was.

"I know where that is," growled Greg. "Let's take a boat ride and have a look-see."

We got back in the truck. "Look, when you get out, walk slowly toward the boat with the big metal thing at the back." He held up a toad-sticker with a ten-inch blade. "I have a knife, and I know how to throw it. If you try to run, you'll be just as dead, only it'll be quieter."

We rode for about ten minutes in silence and pulled up to a marina. In the morning light, I saw a largish, poorly maintained boat with a mailbox hanging off the stern built for pushing overburden out of the way to expose wreckage and treasure on the bottom. I surmised that must be the "big metal thing." I could have ended the party right then and there, but I wanted to wait for the moment I could be sure these lowlifes couldn't hurt anyone else. I was escorted out of the truck at knifepoint. With the knife at my back, I stepped into the boat. I couldn't help but notice Blotto's thirty-foot Conch Cruiser tied up in the next slip. Greg pointed to an ice chest at the stern and I sat down. Ollie proceeded to wrap a rope around me and tie it behind my back. We pulled out of the marina and under US 1, due east facing the morning sun. We motored for about twenty minutes across the Indian River toward Sebastian Inlet, then south. We were running in skinny water that was not much more than ankle-deep to a duck, with sandbars all around. After a while, Greg started pulling on a wetsuit. On the west side of what I assumed to be Smigel Island the boat slowed to a stop and then Ollie dropped the anchor.

"Let's see how much truth there is in your story. I found Matt Black around here a few weeks ago, so I tend to believe you. If I don't find the wreck and that cross, somebody's gonna be very sorry."

"It's a big ocean, Greg, or rather a big river," I answered. "You can't blame me if a wreck's been covered by a hundred and fifty years of sand and mud. You might stumble on some treasure but I promise you won't find any cross."

Greg ignored me and slipped over the side. His partner handed him an underwater metal detector. I sat quietly for about twenty minutes and then couldn't help but notice the tiny red shape of a kayak in the distance to the north, paddling rapidly in our direction. Time to get in position.

"I gotta take a piss," I stated. "Please un-tie me for a minute so I don't piss all over myself. I promise I'll play nice."

Ollie thought for a second. "No funny business," he started. I felt him fumble with the ropes behind my chair and they dropped to the floor. I stood up and saw the forty-four pointed at me. He motioned toward the side of the boat with the pistol.

I walked toward the side of the boat, away from the direction that the kayak was fast approaching. Thankfully, there was an inbound tide, which has to make paddling easier. Ollie dutifully turned toward me, pistol leveled at my chest. I actually relieved myself over the side, making as much noise as possible and taking my time to let Brody quietly approach. The red kayak quietly slid up to the back of the boat. It was Karen's old kayak, which she left behind when she moved back to Oklahoma, noting that kayaking in Oklahoma cow pastures was piss poor. She named it back when she was working a real job and called it, "Sales Calls." She dutifully told her boss at least three times a week she was going out on sales calls, and he never caught on.

With the pistol still pointing at me, Ollie sat down on the side of the boat. Brody slid up behind him without waiting and uppercut with his paddle to chop the pistol into the air. In two steps, I crossed the boat, caught the gun in my hand, and tossed it as far into the Indian River as I could. With my left hand, I hit him flat on the face, jamming his nose into his head. Taking his head in both hands, one quick twist and I heard his neck break with a pop. I let go, and he fell to the deck in a lifeless heap.

Brody leaped out of the kayak and climbed aboard the treasure boat.

"That could have gone wrong, if you had missed. That gun was pointed right at me."

"It was only pointing at your dick," he quipped. "No biggie."

"What kept you?" I joked.

"When I woke up on the morning you disappeared. I got up and had some Cocoa Puffs and a root beer for breakfast, and then noticed you weren't around. Scarlet came in to work and so did the rest of your crew. At first, nobody seemed to think anything was wrong. Scarlet said you sometimes spent the evening in the company of a lady and forgot to come home, said don't give it no mind, and then cooked me a couple of ham and cheese omelets. When you didn't show up the second day we got worried. I asked Scarlet if she noticed anything out of order and she said she didn't see anything strange, just an old chart that was left at the front desk, and handed me the map. When I spread out the chart, the first thing I noticed was that you had circled Smigel Island on the Indian River with a little unhappy face next to it, so I guessed you were in some sort of trouble. I loaded Karen's kayak in my Jeep and came north."

I was happy that my "doodles" had caught Brody's eye. The apple doesn't fall far from the tree. One baddie down and one to go. We pulled '*Sales Calls*' into the boat so Greg wouldn't notice an extra shadow and waited. I rummaged around below decks and dug out a large crescent wrench and a spare weight belt. I looked in the ice chest and downed a bottle of water.

I got through most of a baloney sandwich I found in the ice chest before Gregg's bubbles got close to the boat. He surfaced, handing up the metal detector without looking. I dropped the detector on the deck and went to my knees, leaning over the side of the boat. He still hadn't looked up when I grabbed the back of his scuba tank, spinning him around with my left hand, and swatting the top of his head with the crescent wrench. Before letting him go, I reached around his neck and unzipped his wetsuit. Taking ahold of the necklace and gold coin, I muttered, "This is Matt's" and ripped it off his neck. I let go and he slowly sank out of sight in a pink cloud of blood. Since he was using the metal detector on the ocean floor, he was wearing weights that gave him a slightly negative buoyancy. There are lots of bull sharks that cruise the brackish waters of the Indian River. With any luck, they would follow the blood scent and turn him into shark shit quicker than the crabs would.

I turned to the other thug and hoisted him over the side with the spare weight belt firmly around his waist. He went out of sight a lot quicker.

We pulled up the anchor and motored about two hundred yards toward the other side of the island. Based on the map I saw, Matt predicted the wreck of the *San Miguel* was what *made* Smigel Island. I beached the boat on the island, which was hardly little more than a sand bar. Taking my lead, Brody reached up above the Bimini top and grabbed a fishing rod. He cast the naked hook and sinker out, pretending to fish. Let's see, I had an expensive metal detector and a good knowledge of an untouched wreck's location. It couldn't hurt to poke around a little.

It was like looking for a needle in a haystack on an island full of haystacks. But I already had a pretty good idea I was in the right place. It was a snowball's chance in Hell, but it was the first time hunting treasure in a few years and I had to scratch the itch.

I decided on the unscientific method. I turned to Brody and explained, remembering the story Matt Black told me. "The little island was only a few hundred square yards, and if there was a buried Spanish galleon around, it could be dozens of yards underground. Matt explained to me, when he looked at old charts, there wasn't even an island in the old days." I went on with the theory; "When they opened the Sebastian inlet, the current started to flow, and his guess was that a sandbar started building around the shipwreck." I continued to explain that the biggest clue was the island name Smigel. Probably at one time the old wreck was marked *San Miguel*, which would have been noted S Miguel, and later Americanized, or bastardized, like so many landmarks, to Smigel. A ship that sank three hundred years ago would be not much more than a pile of ballast stones by now. With Brody pretending to fish again I grabbed a snorkel and walked toward the north end of the island with the metal detector and waded in chest-deep. Visibility was about as good as the bottom of a teapot, so I started ranging around with the detector, looking up above water at the boat every once in a while to get my bearings. Matt Black said he estimated treasure, if any, was in about six feet of water, right off the north point of the island. That gave me a pretty narrow search area, less than a few hundred square feet. I spent an hour with no joy, and when halfway through the area, I was rewarded with the "wheep" of a familiar sound. I ran back over the same spot, pinpointing the "wheep." It only took a few moments of brushing away the sand before I saw the unmistakable glint of gold. A gold *Escudo*! It was almost the mate to Greg's necklace save for a little encrustation. One side actually had a date, 1712. I slipped the coin into my pocket. I was still wearing my Columbia shorts, the only clothes I had with me. I guess the baddies planned to make me dead before I needed a change of clothes.

I spent the afternoon covering the area, finding five more Escudos, the top and bottom of a little jewel-studded gold snuff box, and a lump of accretion that probably looked like it had the remains of a flintlock pistol with some silver coins glued to the side.

It was almost dark, and that baloney sandwich hadn't done the trick of satisfying my appetite after two days of forced fasting. I rummaged around the ice chest and dug out some cheese, a length of sausage, and that bottle of Code Rum I had spied in the trailer. "You good with this for dinner?" I asked. "A couple of double cheese burgers, fries, and a root beer would taste a lot better," answered Brody. "Do you think Dominos delivers to this sand bar?" I didn't even grace that question with an honest answer. "You look like missing a meal or two won't hurt you, I want to explore a bit more. Tonight we're campers. Brody gave me a look like he would starve to death before sundown, turned up his nose at the Rum, and rummaged around the island for some dry driftwood. He found a Bic lighter in the toolbox and soon after we had a nice fire. Looking at the fire, I frowned at the smoke and pointed out, "Florida Fish and Wildlife won't be very pleased we built a fire. It's plenty warm. I think you should put it out." Grudgingly, Brody kicked dirt over the driftwood, dragged a couple of dirty towels from the cabin sprayed himself with Off, lay down on the beach sand, and after rolling one of the towels into a pillow, was asleep in ten minutes. I took the other towel, rolled it up, and joined the beach alongside him. My military days made is easy to sleep anywhere. I doused myself with bug spray and dozed off under the stars.

The next morning I was up with the light, and trolled the metal detector over the beach and the shallows up as far as my waist, finding no other sign of treasure. Brody was feigning starvation by ten AM and pleaded we head back. It was time for us to head back towards home and look for some real food. Just before we headed to the marina, I found a flat screwdriver in the toolbox next to the wrench I had used to dispatch Columbus. It still had a little bloody hair stuck to the big end, and I realized my fingerprints and DNA were nicely preserved on the other. I started to reach for the wrench to give it a toss when I had a better Idea. “Put the yak back in the water and climb in,” I told Brody. “Do you think it can get both of us back to the marina?”

“In a pinch, if the waves aren’t too high,” he answered. “Why?”

“Watch. We need to hide the evidence.”

Brody put ‘Sales Calls’ back in the water. I found a set of keys that were laying on the boat’s dash, threw them in a dirty knapsack along with the treasure I had found, and tossed them in the yak. I shoved the boat away from the sand bar, and after safely drifting out a few yards, I fired it up and headed toward the middle of the Indian River. Watching the Garman GPS unit, I idled out until I was about in the middle. The whole darn place is as shallow as a baby bathtub, but I finally ran over a little hole that looked a little deeper. “Thirty-six feet,” I called to Brody, who was trailing me. “Come a little closer,” I called. I shut the motor off, and, taking the screwdriver, I went down the steps to the cabin. I found the hose clamps to the sea water intake. Unscrewing first one, then the other, the hose gave way with a ‘whoosh’ as sea water came rushing in. I dropped the screwdriver and went up the steps topside. The boat was already listing a little. Fortunately, nobody was around to witness the scuttle. After thirty minutes, I motioned Brody alongside, and as the little salvage boat settled into the river, slipping stern-first under the water. I stepped off the transom into the red kayak. Balancing carefully in the middle of the boat, Brody rowed us back to the marina at Micco.

Back at the dock, we beached by the launching ramp, fifty feet from Blotto’s boat. Matt had not taken my advice and chose to berth Blotto’s boat at the closest marina in Micco instead of Fort Pierce as I had suggested. I grimly realized that this area must have been under surveillance and it probably cost him his life, I went over to

Blotto's boat and stepped aboard. I put one of the gold coins I found on the island in the package tray under a towel, hoping Blotto got back to his boat before anyone else did. We walked up the ramp to the truck. We tried the keys I found in the truck that brought me here. As expected, the keys unlocked the door. I opened the glove box and found a cell phone, along with my loaded Glock I had loaned Matt Black and the title to the truck along with a half dozen grungy Mcdonald's napkins. Hmm, well, one Gregory Columbus had no need for his wheels anymore. I called Rumpy and told him the Reader's Digest version of what happened. I also told him where Blotto's boat was.

"Tell him to come pick it up." I advised, and send me the bill for any dockage, damage, or gas and I'll reimburse him." Then I remembered. "Oh tell him to come soon so the little 'thank you' bonus I left in the tray doesn't end up in someone else's pocket."

We hit the Outrigger Bar for a few cheeseburgers then headed north in Greg's truck, taking our time on the way. I crawled up onto US 95, avoiding the hated turnpike. The highway, which starts all the way up in New Brunswick Canada, rather unceremoniously dumps you off onto US 1 in Coconut Grove and south to Florida City. Coming out of Florida City, I chose Card Sound Road instead of the Seventeen Mile stretch, It's more scenic, always has less traffic, and has my favorite pit stop on the way, namely Alabama Jacks. Regardless of the burgers he wolfed down, Brody licked his lips in anticipation of some 'real' food. I ordered a fried shrimp basket, chasing mine with a cold Bud longneck. It tasted exquisite.

Brody? Two more plain cheeseburgers of course. I asked my son if he wanted to start with a salad and he shook his head vigorously. "That's not food, dad, that's what food eats." When we got our order, I casually tossed a few fries into the canal and watched the dinner-plate size Mangrove Snappers that always hung out around the dock attack them as aggressively as Brody wolfed down his lunch. (I always wondered if those Snappers, fixtures at Jacks for generations, had high cholesterol from eating too much fried shrimp tails and fries.)

"Did you know this was Jimmy Buffet's first keys experience?" I explained to Brody around a mouthful of hushpuppy. "He was living in Coconut Grove and down to his last dime when Jerry Jeff Walker decided to take a little road trip, bringing Jimmy and Jerry's wife along for the ride. I guess the first place they stopped was Alabama Jacks. Needless to say, he fell in love with the life and the lifestyle and has been writing songs about these islands ever since." Brody nodded through his cheeseburger, halfheartedly paying attention – He was weary of my Jimmy Buffet stories and I don't think he ever listened to a Buffet song that I wasn't force-feeding him.

We cruised leisurely up the keys, passing what was left of Anne's beach, totally destroyed by the hurricane. "It's gonna be years until the keys come all the way back," I remarked. Looking at the lost facilities at Anne's beach, Brody answered, "maybe never."

Late that afternoon, we pulled up in front of Nobody's Inn in the pickup. The crew hardly looked up. Though I didn't vanish very often, they didn't show much surprise that I was AWOL for two and a half days. I threw up my arms in mock surrender. "Don't pay the ransom, I escaped!" I shouted to nobody in particular. I guess I need to come home minus a body part or something before anyone would take notice. Everything at the Inn appeared to be running smoothly. Scarlet called from the front desk. "What, you want a day named after you? Get in here and bake tomorrow's bread. You can't 'spect me to do everything."

Ah it's good to be home.

I walked up to the front door. Out front, Marcus was trimming the huge philodendron in the front yard. I turned and walked back toward him.

"Do you have a driver's license?" I asked the burly gardener.

"I have a license, suh, but I can't afford a car so's I walk to work every day. I don need one anyways."

I tossed him a set of keys. "Here, that's yours," I motioned to the truck. "I found the title in the console. You can change it to your name. I might suggest you paint it, but for some reason, I don't think the current owner will come looking for it. Or, if you want a few bucks, you can drive it up to Miami and sell it off to one of your homies and have it hauled off to Saint Somewhere. I don't really care."

I stepped over Cousin Eddie, sound asleep in the foyer. He didn't even grace me with a tail-wag. Brody went off to raid the fridge for vittles, and I headed upstairs for a well-earned shower.

The world was at peace again.

Neither Brody nor I could stand the possibility of a mostly un-salvaged eighteenth-century Spanish galleon sitting out there untouched. Despite it being inside a preserve, we sneaked away a few more times and went 'fishing' on Smigel. We contacted Blotto through Rumpy and he happily offered to rent his boat again, based on the 'tip' we left in the package tray last time - I stepped into the boat. Knowing well the value of a gold doubloon I scoffed at the offer. "I don't want to buy that tub, just use it for a few days." Blotto grudgingly accepted the going rate, namely six hundred a week, plus gas, with the island only being a mile or two from Micco, I asked him to trailer it back to the marina there which he also agreed to. We cruised out to the island and set up camp for a few days every few weeks, usually on a Monday or Tuesday, when snooping boat traffic and the Florida Fish and Wildlife presence was at a minimum. Brody continued to fish, only this time he wasn't pretending. He brought his cast-net along and after a few expert tosses he netted a small bucket full of finger mullet. That stretch of water had little or no fishing pressure, and while I was scouting for treasure, Brody boated some nice redfish, a few snook, and hooked a hungry bull shark that had to be at least seven feet long. It spooled his reel, and then broke off, resulting in a trip to the tackle store for some stronger line. It also reminded me to stay on my toes in this chocolate milk-colored river.

I prospected again along the shore and surrounding flats, covering most of the area when I was in the clear to search, paying close attention to avoid being watched by passing pleasure riders on houseboats and fishing boats along with the occasional FWC patrol. The *San Miguel* must have been carrying minimum treasure, which didn't match up according to Matt Black. The ship's manifests located in the historical archives in Seville Spain said it contained a huge cargo of silver, gold, imported china from the Far East, and that elusive cross. More likely, it had either been salvaged by the

Spanish in the years immediately following the hurricane, was buried deep underground by centuries of wave action, or was scattered across a debris field halfway between here and Fort Pierce. I found a few more gold coins and a few other unidentified items but it was slim pickings. Since we couldn't bring in any heavy equipment, we left the site in pristine condition and will take the secret of the lost *San Miguel* to our grave. On the upside, I got some quality time with my son, who had grown up to become quite a man.

Flashback - 1741

In 1741, the English invaded Cuba in a war called the *War of Jenkins' Ear* with Spain. Edward Vernon, the British admiral who devised the scheme, saw his occupying troops lose to local guerrilla resistance, and more critically, an epidemic, forcing him to withdraw his fleet to British-owned Jamaica. In the War of the Austrian Succession, the British carried out unsuccessful attacks against Santiago de Cuba in 1747 and again in 1748. Additionally, a skirmish between British and Spanish naval squadrons occurred near Havana in 1748.

The Seven Years' War, which erupted in 1754 across three continents, eventually arrived in the Spanish Caribbean. Spain's alliance with the French pitched them into direct conflict with the British, and in 1762 a British expedition of five warships and four thousand troops set out from Portsmouth to capture Cuba. The British arrived in June, and by August had Havana under siege. When Havana surrendered, the admiral of the British fleet, entered the city as a conquering new governor and took control of the whole western part of the island. The arrival of the British immediately opened up trade with their North American and Caribbean colonies, causing a rapid transformation of Cuban society. Food, horses, and other goods flooded into the city, and thousands of slaves from West Africa were transported to the island to work on the under-staffed sugar plantations.

Though Havana, which had become the third-largest city in the Americas, was to enter an era of sustained development and closed ties with North America during this period, the British occupation of the city proved short-lived. Pressure from London's sugar merchants fearing a decline in sugar prices forced a series of negotiations with the Spanish over colonial territories. Less than a year after Havana was seized, the Peace of Paris was signed by the three warring powers, ending the Seven Years' War. The treaty gave Britain all of Florida in exchange for Cuba on France's recommendation to Spain. The French advised that declining the offer could result in Spain losing Mexico and much of the South American mainland to the British. This led to disappointment in

Britain, as many believed that Florida was a poor return for Cuba and Britain's other gains in the war.

Havana became the principal port and naval base for all of Hispanic America and existed solely for the good of the mother country. Havana was the capital of the New World. Trade with countries other than Spain was prohibited and all shipping had to be done with Spanish ships. Almost all ships would put into Havana for food and water before returning to Europe and the only practical route was northward via the Gulf Stream. This explains why so many ships in the waters off the Florida Keys were dashed against the shallow reefs.

The English or Spanish ownership of the keys was never really settled. The English Governor Ogilvie said the keys were part of Florida. Spanish agent Elixio said that they were The Martires or Havana Norte and were a part of Cuba, and not Florida; therefore not part of the treaty, which had not defined the boundaries of Florida. Both countries stood by their positions; however, neither contested the issue other than with words.

With Florida under English rule, many of the Spanish in Florida moved back to Cuba, as did the Spanish in Santo Domingo when it was ceded to France. Thousands more fled from French Haiti to Cuba when the blacks revolted and assumed power in Haiti. As a result, Cuba's population grew while Florida was under English control, and Cuban commerce with the U.S. increased.

A census of Cuba in 1774 indicated a total population of 161,670 and by 1817 it had grown to 553,033. Havana's population of 70,000 had surpassed that of early New York City. Secessionist movements broke out in 1809 and continued off and on.

In 1815, the Spanish governor of Cuba in Havana deeded the island of Key West to Juan Pablo Salas, an officer of the Royal Spanish Navy Artillery posted in Saint Augustine, Florida. After Florida was transferred to the United States in 1821, Salas was so eager to sell the island that he sold it twice. First, he traded the island for a sloop valued at $575 to General John Geddes, the former governor of South Carolina, and then to U.S. businessman John W. Simonton, during a meeting in a Havana café on January 19, 1822, for the equivalent of $2,000 in pesos. Geddes tried in vain to secure his rights to the property before Simonton who, with the aid of some influential friends in Washington, was able to gain clear title to the island. Simonton had wide-ranging business interests in Mobile, Alabama. He bought the island because a friend, John Whitehead, had drawn his attention to the opportunities presented by the island's strategic location.

John Whitehead had been stranded in Key West after a shipwreck in 1819 and he had been impressed by the potential offered by the deep harbor of the island. The island was indeed considered the "Gibraltar of the West" because of its strategic location on the 90-mile wide and deep shipping lane between the Atlantic Ocean and the Gulf of Mexico.

On March 25, 1822, Lt. Commander Matthew C. Perry sailed the schooner *Shark* to Key West and planted the U.S. flag, claiming the keys as United States property. No protests were made over the American claim on Key West, and so the Florida Keys became the property of the United States.

After claiming the Florida Keys for the United States, Perry renamed *Cayo Hueso* (for its original description as the island of bones) to Thompson's Island for Secretary of the Navy Smith Thompson, and the harbor Port Rodgers in honor of War of 1812 hero and President of the Navy Supervisors Board John Rodgers. In 1823, Commodore David Porter of the United States Navy West Indies Anti-Pirate Squadron took charge of Key West, where he ruled as a military dictator under martial law. Porter was tasked by the American Navy to end acts of piracy in the Key West area, including the lucrative slave ship trade.

Cuba failed to prosper during this period due to Spanish trade regulations. Spain had set up a trade monopoly in the Caribbean, and their primary objective was to protect trade, which they did by barring the islands from trading with any foreign ships. The resultant stagnation of economic growth was particularly pronounced in Cuba because of its great strategic importance in the Caribbean, and the stranglehold that Spain kept on it as a result.

As soon as Spain opened Cuba's ports up to foreign ships, a great sugar boom began that lasted until the 1880s. The island was perfect for growing sugar, being dominated by rolling plains, with rich soil and adequate rainfall. By 1860, all of Cuba was devoted to growing sugar, having to import all other necessary goods. Cuba was particularly dependent on the United States, which bought most of its sugar. In 1820, Spain abolished the slave trade, hurting the Cuban economy even more and forcing planters to buy more expensive, illegal, and troublesome slaves (as demonstrated by the slave rebellion on the Spanish ship *Amistad* in 1839).

A former colonel in the Royal Spanish Army, Narcisso Lopez, fled to the U.S. in 1849 under suspicion of overthrowing the Spanish government. He quickly gathered support against the Spanish oppression of the local Cubans, but his first liberating invasion of Cuba from U.S. soil failed. He quickly organized another invasion party of about 450 sympathizers and landed at Cardenas, Cuba. Lopez did not have the support of the local Cuban citizens and had to return to Key West in failure. It was not yet time for a large-scale Cuban revolt. Spanish/Cuban relations festered, and in 1868, Cuba's longest and bloodiest war, the Ten Years' War, started. The war produced 200,000 Cuban and Spanish combined casualties. In addition, there was great property damage. Many prominent Cubans fled to Key West. This is also known as the Great Thirty Year War as it effectively continued to 1898.

Vicente Martinez Ybor, a Cuban exile, opened a cigar factory, the El Principe de Gales, in Key West. (This marked the beginning of Havana cigar manufacturing in the U.S.) The San Carlos Institute was dedicated in Key West on January 21, 1871. Named after Carlos M. de Cespedes. Cespedes, a distinguished lawyer, and Cuban planter, was one of the first to issue the cry of "Cuba Libre" in 1868. His son was elected mayor of Key West in 1876. Key West became a political-financial center that supported civil unrest in Cuba. The U.S. did not intervene, as it was recovering from its own Civil War in 1865.

11
Legs

Normally I don't have anything to do with regular check-ins. I leave that to Scarlet, who sits at the check-in desk almost seven days a week – Scarlet's choice, not my instruction, so I was surprised when she sought me out in the kitchen one morning.

"Got the munchies?" I asked. She ignored the smart-assed remark.

"Boss, there's an Amazon out in front that says she wants to stay for two months."

"If the plastic's good, I'm okay with that," I answered. "Does she know this ain't an extended stay place?" I asked. "It's gonna cost someplace on the north side of six grand a month, and my cooking's gonna get a little boring. I'm not that inventive."

"I pre-authorized the card," Scarlet answered, "and it's good."

Amazon? I thought. I like big girls. "Maybe I should take a look-see." I took my apron off and sauntered out to the lobby. With Eddie at his usual spot, flaked out on the floor, sitting at the check-in was our guest.

"Russel Philipps," I extended a hand.

She stood up and returned my handshake with a firm, almost masculine handshake.

"Judy Long," she said in a soft, deep voice. Tranny? I don't think so. I've known Scarlet for years, and I've learned almost every subtle way to twig my gaydar. She almost seemed to stumble on the name, like she just made it up or "borrowed" it. I filed that thought in the back of my head under 'useless knowledge you never know you might need.' The plastic was good and that's good enough for me.

Without being overly obvious, I gave her the once-over. Maybe six feet tall, about one-sixty. Nice, firm rack. Conservative capri denims, sandals, and a sleeveless pull-over. Medium tan and no visible tattoos. It looked like she was wearing one of those long-line Maidenform bras that were popular in the fifties. Any more modest and she would be in a nun's habit. She wore longish fire red hair, and I was pretty sure it was from her heritage and not a bottle. There aren't many girls nowadays days fuss with that much hair. Amazing eyes so green I suspected contacts, but it didn't fit the rest of her conservative appearance. The only visible admission to fashion were dark green painted fingers and toes. She wasn't wearing any makeup, and had no visible jewelry, although she sported multiple holes in her ears, like she was hiding a checkered past.

The way she was balanced on the balls of her feet like a cat ready to pounce, she looked ready to rumble. She looked confident and self-assured, and I could tell she could take care of herself. There was no doubt in my mind that any guy that made an unwelcome pass on her was still looking for his co*jones.*

I was instantly in love, or at least lust, but something told me I'd never get to first base with this one.

"So I hear you want to stay for a few months. You're gonna get tired of the menu. I'm not that good of a cook," I ventured.

"A little yogurt, a muffin, and some fruit for breakfast, and I'm happy," she answered. "I just need to hang out and recharge my batteries for a while."

"I can relate to that," I responded, nodding. "Tough time on the job?"

"Something like that," Judy returned, vaguely. She didn't elaborate.

I couldn't think of anything else brilliant to say, so I nodded "good" to Scarlet and ducked back into the kitchen.

And that's about how it went. Breakfast every morning, as she promised. Yogurt, muffin fresh fruit, hot tea, and a glass of grapefruit juice. I might run into her during the day, poolside, reading a trashy novel, sitting in partial shade in a plain-Jane conservative one-piece bathing suit, or more likely Bermuda shorts and a ribbed tank-top with wide shoulder straps. She never took advantage of the clothing-optional policy and didn't have much to do with those that did. She usually went out during the evening, always leaving after dark and returning by herself before two.

I would have given a week's pay to peek under that armor.

Flashback - 1866

Broderick Sawyer was a member of one of the most influential and wealthy families in the Florida Keys. They came to the keys from the Bahamas in the latter half of the nineteenth century as British loyalists, fleeing from American rule after the Revolutionary War, and became proficient as wreckers. The Sawyers and several other families got rich from the countless ships that went aground on the treacherous Keys' reefs. The family branched out, investing in imports and exports, bringing cattle from the East Coast of the US and transporting them to Punta Rasa near present-day Fort Meyers in Southwest Florida. They also traded sugar, rum, and tobacco from Cuba, shipping sugar and rum to the East Coast, and eventually bringing tobacco directly to Key West to make cigars. Young Broderick had a nose for business from an early age, and after attending several colleges in New York and Pennsylvania, assumed the helm of the family business by mid-century. As one of Key West's most prominent citizens, he acquired a piece of property on Simonton Street and built a modest unassuming single-story home on the lot mostly from timber salvaged from wrecked ships. Along with the house he had rough slave quarters constructed at the rear of the property. He married into another prominent conch family and fathered three children. Never a great father or doting husband, his wife died of 'accidental' poisoning in the early 1870's.

His close ties to the Cuban tobacco and sugar business, the latter both for refined sugar and the lucrative rum business meant he visited the island frequently. He knew which political hands to grease with *mordida* (bribe money) and became a respected visitor, especially at the Galarza Plantation. He contracted sugar, rum, and tobacco, the latter for the cigar factories in Key West, two of which he owned himself, and several others, owned and manned by transplanted Cuban *patrons.*

The Galarza family continued to grow their plantation over the years, becoming richer and more powerful throughout the seventeen and eighteen hundreds. The emerald and ruby crusted cross became a family heirloom, gracing the neck of every family matriarch for over a hundred and fifty years, and made a most attractive wedding dowry, but the family always ensured that if it left the plantation around the neck of a blushing bride, it always eventually returned home, usually in the possession of a grieving widow. Since women couldn't own land and any property in the possession of their husbands fell to a brother or uncle. More likely, a daughter would marry a rich suitor into the Galazara family, keeping her jewels around her neck and adding her husband's wealth to the family. Galazara women always outlived their husbands, driving them to an early grave literally by nagging them to death.

Why did they die first? Because they *wanted* to.

During his frequent visits, Sawyer became acquainted with one of the youngest Galarza daughters, Louisa, first as a gawky headstrong child with raven hair and flashy dark eyes, then a blooming teenager, and finally a radiant, unruly, beauty. Wild and free, she was often seen around the dockside cantinas, drinking, smoking cigars, and hanging around various shipmasters.

Then, suddenly, she was gone one day. Broderick inquired first at the Galarza Plantation, where he was met with quiet silence, and sideways glances. Around the cantinas, he learned that she had become entangled with one of the ship's captains, and had managed to become pregnant.

According to local scuttlebutt, the Galarza family, looking to escape scandal, whisked Louisa off to a convent on the *Isle De Mujers* on the southwest coast. Sawyer didn't see her for over a year and forgot about her after that.

Then one day on a visit to the plantation, he caught a flash of dark hair in the hall. Louisa had matured into the most amazing beauty. She caught a glimpse of Sawyer, nearly forty years her senior, and coyly vanished down the hall with a tiny smile. Broderick looked her way with admiration; he hoped to see her again during his visit.

He saw her two nights later while attending a formal feast in his honor recognizing the many decades of a mutually beneficial business relationship. He was astonished with his luck the beauty was assigned to sit next to him at the dinner table. She looked radiant in a green silk dress, cut low in the front and adorned with a massive, jewel-encrusted gold cross. She had little to say throughout dinner and gave the distinct impression that she would rather be someplace else. Anyplace else. The senior Galarza, sitting directly across the table from Sawyer, kept a lively conversation going all night, frequently pointing out his daughter's beauty, wit, and charm. It finally came to Broderick before the evening was done; this young beauty was being presented to the widower, his wife having died, only two years earlier.

After dinner, as was the custom, the men retired to the library for after dinner drinks and cigars. The elder Galarza strategically placed himself next to Sawyer and began a conversation.

"This island is too small for my daughter," he started. "I think she needs to see a little more of the world. I was thinking of sending her to school in *Nuevo York*, but there may be a closer resolution."

Sawyer slowly puffed on his cigar. He fairly well knew what was coming. He was about to be asked to become a godfather and protector to the unruly young woman and take her under his wing as a ward in Key West for the next several years. He completely misunderstood the plan and was literally astonished when he heard the elder Galarza voice his proposal.

"I would like you to take Louisa's hand in marriage."

The old man was astonished. "But I'm nearly sixty," he blurted out.

"Marriage is a young man's folly and an old man's comfort," Galarza gently explained. "It's not the same for young, irresponsible girls. It's best that she go under the protection of an experienced guide. You are recently widowed. This scenario is best for both of you, in more ways than one."

Sawyer nodded gravely. No need to mention that his first wife died by mysterious means. "I will do my best to be a faithful husband," he said solemnly.

"There's no need for you to be that gentle," Galarza cautioned. "Louisa will be a handful. *Un gato ardpara to bajo el porche.* She's a hard cat to keep under the porch."

Broderick Sawyer returned to Key West ahead of his reluctant bride by two years, determined to make her the nicest home south of Savannah. He hastily ordered his small home torn down and hired the island's best craftsmen to build a true mansion, complete with six bedrooms, a reading room, a kitchen, and a huge parlor with a crystal chandelier. Three stories tall, to catch the afternoon breezes, it sported a large widow's walk, and when finished graced Key West with some of the finest architecture on the island. The back yard sported a stable and carriage barn, and a large banyan tree loomed over the lush vegetable garden. Despite the recommendation by Marcus, the gardener that Sawyer should remove the tree to let more light in, his love of the massive limbs kept it in place. "Let it stand," said the old man. "We can always buy more cabbage, but when that banyan tree is gone, there will never be a replacement."

The mansion was huge but mostly vacant. Although the Sawyer family made up a substantial part of the island's population, Broderick Sawyer, one of the wealthiest men in town paid little tribute to the other comfortable relatives nearby. They all owned substantial homes in town and learned to distance themselves from the ruthless business dealings of the elder Sawyer. To call him a miserly scrooge would have been a compliment.

PONTIAC

12
No Joy

After a few weeks of trying every angle possible on Judy, I just gave up on that fantasy. I figured I was reading National Geographic, looking at places I was never going to visit. I more or less forgot her, running into her around the house, greeted each time with a polite, but cold, smile. Despite my efforts, I couldn't even drag her into a conversation, much less the sack.

So be it.

Then one day, the shit hit the proverbial fan. It started just after breakfast with Scarlet yelling from the lobby.

"Boss, you better come here!" she called. I laid my apron on the table and walked up to the reception desk.

"I just got a call from Amex," she started. "I ran Miss Judy Long's card for another week and it came back unauthorized. I suspect we're going to get a charge-back for all the previous charges too."

"Stolen?" I asked

"Hotter than the hinges on the gates of hell," Scarlet answered. "The owner is some rich lady in the Midwest and had so much plastic she didn't miss the card or her I.D. It wasn't until she got the bill that she noticed it missing."

I looked upstairs with a frown. "I haven't seen 'Miss Long' all morning. She didn't even show up for her breakfast," I commented. "Reckon I better go tap on her door."

"Don't bother, boss," Bela spoke as he walked up behind me. "She just ripped off you Firebird."

This just got deadly serious. My 1977 black Pontiac Firebird Trans-Am was my pride and joy and a Smokey and the Bandit look alike, right down to the gold eagle on the hood and the removable T-tops. It was a match to my ex-girlfriend Maggie's Firebird, only a little newer. I'd had it restored frame-up to nine points and worth more than some houses. Most of the time it just sat in the garage out back gathering dust, but I pulled it out every month or so to blow the cobwebs out (both me and the Firechicken), give it a bath, and keep the battery charged.

"How long ago?" I asked, reaching in my pocket for my cell phone.

"Two minutes," Bela answered. "I saw her pull out of the garage. She looked like she was heading north."

I dialed a number on my cell. "Rumpy, where are you?" I asked.

"I just happen to be in town." John Rumpendorfer drawled. "A little banking this morning. I came by Wells Fargo to visit my money."

"Come get me now, quick like," I responded. "A guest just ripped off my Firebird."

"On my way," Rumpy answered. I appreciated he didn't ask twenty questions. "Did you call the cops?"

"It would take them the whole day for them to get organized." I came back. "Besides, I don't want this cow arrested. I want to deal with this personally."

While Rumpy was on the way, I beat it upstairs to my man-cave to get my phone and some cash. I was stunned to see the "secret" entrance to my private room was standing wide open. I walked into the room and opened the drawer to the nightstand, where I kept my wallet and other valuables. It was gone, as was that very special gold doubloon that once belonged to Matt Black, along with the rest of my treasure I had accumulated, and my dad's old K-Bar pocket knife. I was hot before. Now I'm really pissed. Then I heard a car stop out front and a horn honked. Rumpy was pulling up in his Four Runner. I ran down the steps and called to Bela, "How much?" Bela knew what I was asking and looked at his watch. He was the only person in the world I knew who didn't own a cell phone and *did* own a watch. A real Timex Ironman Triathlon. "Twenty-one and a half minutes!" he called out.

Maybe there was just enough time to head her off at the pass.

I jumped in the right seat and yelled, "Step on it!" and we roared off like a heard of turtles.

"We're not gonna catch her at this speed!" I yelled, "You gotta bust the speed limit by at least ten!"

Rumpy increased the speed a tiny fraction. He looked at me.

"Do the math," he exclaimed. "With a twenty-minute lead, we don't have a chance of catching her before she gets to Florida City. If she gets past there, she can pick her getaway route."

I did some calculations in my head. "The last time, I took a drive; I parked the Firebird with less than a quarter tank," I answered. "She's gotta stop for gas, and since the plastic bounced this morning, she knows she has to pay cash. There were plenty of bucks in my wallet that she just ripped off. I'm guessing she'll stop at the Big Coppit Circle K and if it's the same cashier that was there the last time I stopped, it will take at least ten minutes to fill up after she takes her time visiting with the trailer trash that's buying a six-pack of Busch and a Slim Jim for breakfast and making her next Saturday night skank date. That takes it down to ten minutes. If we bust the speed limit by ten miles per hour, figuring ten-per it will keep you under the Monroe County Sherriff's radar. I'm guessing that she doesn't know that unwritten rule and will drive the posted limit all the way to Homestead. We should catch her sometime just after the Marathon. How much motion-lotion you got?"

Rumpy nodded and obediently eased the Toyota up a little past fifty-five. "Filled her up this morning." He answered, looking at the gas gauge. "We can get to the Georgia line before we need a fill-up. My bladder won't last as long as the fuel in the tank."

"That Firebird can't," I answered. "It will pass anything but a gas station."

"And if we don't catch her by Florida City?" Rumpy asked.

"Then my baby will end up on blocks with no motor in some chop-shop in Opa-Locka," I answered glumly. "So we gotta try."

"Then try we must!" Rumpy answered.

Flashback- July 7, 1865 – Lincolnton, Georgia

An excerpt from Book Number 1 Treasure Keys

Albert Sawyer, a former lieutenant in the Confederate Army, lay quietly on a bluff overlooking the road between Lincolnton and Irwinville Georgia. Below, he watched a company of Union Calvary move past. The war was over; he truly wanted no contact with what he still considered the enemy. As they moved out of sight around the bend, he motioned behind him for the ex-Confederate soldiers to move up with the horse-drawn wagon. The wagon appeared to only have a load of hay, but the horses strained up the low hill, and the wagon tracks bit deeply into the thick red Georgia clay. They eased the wagon back onto the road and quietly drove toward the Mumford Ranch in Brantley County.

Arriving near dusk, Sawyer pulled the wagon into the old livery stable. The elderly black attendant unhitched the horses, pulled water from the well, and tended to the team. Slavery was over, but there was still a definite line between served and former servants in the south. Under lantern light, the soldiers unloaded the hay and removed the floorboards of the wagon, exposing several heavy canvas bags full of gold and silver coins. Six large lead ingots were also laid at the bottom of the wagon. The lead ingots, which were originally destined to be melted into bullets, weighed over 50 pounds each and were topped with an oval design with the classic "CSA" emblem, denoting the Confederate States of America.

"What are we doing with those?" asked one of the sergeants. "That wagon is heavy enough. They were all around President Davis' mansion," replied Sawyer. "They were being used for doorstops. I brought them along because I think they might have some value because of where they were during the war."

Choosing a place in the corner of the barn, the soldiers dug a deep hole and dropped the bags in. The coins, valued at over $200,000 US dollars, were part of a cache that had been traveling with Confederate President Jefferson Davis and his cabinet when they fled Richmond ahead of advancing union troops earlier that month. Davis had entrusted Sawyer, a Key West native and loyal

Confederate, with a good part of the half-million dollars in gold and silver. Some of this had come from banks in Richmond and the remainder was on loan from England. Part of the gold bullion was comprised of treasure captured from Spanish salvage vessels by English privateers over 100 years earlier. This gold, identifiable by its rough cast and Spanish "chop" marks, was not with the wagon and had seemingly vanished months earlier. After covering the bullion, they erased signs of their work and covered the corner in hay and straw. Exhausted, the squad bedded down for the evening.

The following morning, leaving the lead ingots, their pistols, rifles, and a small leather bag of English gold sovereigns in the bottom of the wagon, they replaced the false-floor, hitched up the team, and headed south for a four-day trip to Savannah. Now dressed in civilian clothes, they successfully gave the impression to any Union troops that they were ex-soldiers and poor farmers making their way toward the city. With all arms hidden beneath the floorboards with the lead ingots and carrying nothing of value, they were able to successfully talk their way through any Union opposition. Only once did it appear they might be arrested, and they averted it only when Sawyer quietly pressed an English gold sovereign into the palm of the Union Lieutenant. The last night before arriving in Savannah, they camped far off the road, ate in silence, and bedded down for the night. Well before daybreak, the quiet was broken by the sound of four quick pistol shots.

Sawyer drove the wagon alone into the city of Savannah, Georgia. William Tecumseh Sherman's army had occupied Savannah until January of 1865 when they moved north into the Carolinas. They had treated the city mildly when it was occupied a few months earlier. The city and infrastructure remained fairly intact, despite the port being closed during the war due to the blockade, and all rail lines in and out of the city having been destroyed. Shipping was beginning to resume in the port as the trade-starved city started to come back to life. Sawyer found his uncle's house, and, after unhitching the wagon, led the team to a livery stable and boarded them. He advised the owner they were for sale. That night he quietly pulled the boards from the false bottom of the wagon, hid the firearms under the house, and stacked the six lead bars in a corner of the kitchen.

The following morning, Sawyer walked to the industrial part of town near the river. After some searching, he found the building he was looking for, a former button factory that was, in all appearances, closed down. Pushing open the unlocked door, he saw a single kerosene light toward the back of the building. "I'm looking for Hans Kraker," Sawyer called out. "I'm Kraker," a voice responded in a thick German accent. "What is it you want?"

"I heard from a mutual friend you can plate things with gold," Sawyer replied. "Who told you this?" Kraker asked. "Let's just say Mr. Davis sent me."

His eyes narrowed, and he answered slowly. "Yes, I have a small foundry, and I plated buttons and buckles with nickel for the confederacy," said Kraker. "I can plate with gold too. What do you need me to do? I still have the chemicals, but little material."

"I have some lead bars that I need to turn into gold bars, with no questions asked," Sawyer replied.

"Hmmm, this is not easy to do. Gold does not stick to lead, so you have to plate the lead with something that will stick to lead and use something that will stick to gold. For that, you use nickel, which I have some of, but I have no gold."

"I can provide the gold, and you can keep whatever you don't use for plating as payment. Is that acceptable?"

"How much gold do you have?"

"Thirty English sovereigns."

"And how much lead do you need to plate?"

Sawyer held out his hands to indicate the size of the lead bars. "Six bars, about this size." Kraker thought for a moment, knowing he wouldn't need the gold from more than three of the half-ounce gold coins to effectively plate the bars, but Sawyer wouldn't know that. "I need forty coins, nothing less," responded Kraker. "Okay," replied Sawyer. "I'll give you five more if you can get it done by the weekend. I need to ship them someplace."

"Very well," replied Kraker. "Bring them to me tonight with your gold. Use the back door through the alley. Make sure no one follows you."

Later that evening, Sawyer made six trips to the foundry,

carrying one lead bar at a time. On the last trip Sawyer also brought the bag of English coins and handed them over to the metal smith. The plating area smelled strongly of chemicals, and Kraker worked with large leather gloves and a heavy apron. "You had best leave," Kraker said to Sawyer. "These chemicals are extremely strong and dangerous unless you are careful and wear the correct clothing. Come back Friday with a wagon and we will be done."

Metal electroplating has been in existence for nearly 2000 years. Using a substance like potassium cyanide that creates a weak electrical current, metals can be plated. The chemicals are poisonous and harsh, and the lung-damaging fumes can result in a short lifespan. Kraker had learned from his Russian "Volga Deutsch" Jewish ancestors and worked with a heavy mask over his nose and mouth. First placing the lead bars in the solution, he dipped the nickel anodes in the bath and left them to soak for two days. Cranking them up out of the vat, the lead bars had transformed into the bright silvery color of nickel. This "strike" would enable them to now accept a gold finish. He then attached three of the gold Sovereigns to wires and replaced the nickel-coated bars into another chemical bath. This time the bars were left in the solution for four days as the coins gave up metal volume and the bars slowly turned gold. Late Friday morning, he pulled them out of the solution a final time and rinsed them in a bath of fresh running well water. The lead bars were now gold bars. They would pass even the most careful examination, and the plating was thick enough that it would not flake off. The lead bars were heavy to start with, and it was likely no one would have ever picked up a lead or gold bar of that size, so the illusion was believable. Kraker carefully hid the remaining gold coins, and when Sawyer arrived that afternoon in his wagon, he accepted the bonus solemnly.

"You can promise nobody has seen you plating these bars?" Sawyer asked. "I live alone, and I work alone," Kraker replied. "I have had no employees for nearly a year."

As Kraker turned to go back into his foundry, he never had a chance to react to the butt of a .36 caliber Navy revolver. He slumped to the ground unconscious. It took Sawyer some effort, but he was able to drag Kraker back into the plating room, and, being careful not to create a splash, rolled the body into the vat of potassium cyanide, where his body became unrecognizable in minutes.

Dead men tell no tales.

Faro Blanco, Marathon Key

12
Chase

We flashed past the Big Coppit Shell station, and I resisted the temptation to stop and verify my guess. We went on through Sugarloaf, past Boondocks on Ramrod Key, and throttled down for Big Pine, less we send some unsuspecting Key Deer to Valhalla, and end up filling out reams of forms with Florida Highway Patrol, along with paying a hefty fine and jail time. Then we pretty well-lit it up over Bahia Honda and the Seven Mile Bridge, waving the obligatory salute to Fred the Tree on the way. Again we backed down to the thirty-five miles per hour posted limit as we cleared the permanent speed trap at the end of the bridge. As we started to pick it up again, out of the corner of my eye I saw a familiar black shape in the side parking lot of the Hyatt Place. "Stop!" I yelled. Rump jumped on the brakes and turned left as I pointed. Sure enough, there was my Trans-Am. Rumpy hardly pulled to a stop and I jumped out. "See you back in town," I waved.

"Don't you want me to wait?" Rumpy asked.

"No need," I answered. "One way or the other, I'll be driving my own car back."

Rumpy shrugged, and turned around, heading back toward Key West. I checked my car. It looked fine. The exhaust was still ticking from heat. Wherever she was, it wasn't far.

I went into the lobby and approached the front desk. "Did the person driving that Firebird just check in?" I asked.

"We're not allowed to give out customer information," the agent replied blandly. "Besides I don't know what car you're talking about. I don't drive." He quipped with a slight lisp. "I can't tell one car from another."

With no other clues, I shrugged and walked through the hotel past the outdoor pool to the Faro Blanco tiki bar out back by the marina. It had been quite a while since Karen and I stayed here but nothing had changed. There was a nice outdoor bar, a bistro with a view of the marina, and a pool stocked with well-tanned thong-backed beauties and two dozen screaming kids. Overall, I rate Faro Blanco among one the finest locations in the keys. I scanned the bar, and there she was. I almost didn't recognize her. Gone was he demure, conservative girl. In her place was a gorgeous vision with a fiery unleashed mop, and she was dressed in a white thin spaghetti strap tank top and classy short, faded denim cutoffs. The platform wedge sandals made her six-plus foot height even taller. I could see a tribal "tramp stamp" peeking out from the bottom of her top above the shorts. Not that there was a lot of competition sitting at the bar, but the rest of the talent knew they were hopelessly outclassed by this package. Three pimply-faced pre-teens entered into instant puberty, two single guys had premature ejaculations, and four chubby, senior citizen tourists immediately started calculating their net worth, contemplating the very unlikely possibility of arranging concubinage, much to the displeasure of their equally rotund spouses. Ignoring the various chicken dances, I found an open seat next to her and plopped down. The waitress approached and I said in a fairly loud voice, "I'll have what she's having." I don't know what kind of reaction I was expecting, a jump or maybe she would rabbit.

She didn't even flinch.

"Okay, one Yukon Jack and beer back." The server announced and turned.

"I never saw you drink anything stronger than green tea," I remarked. "Lifestyle change?"

She took a sip of the Jack and washed it down with the beer. "I suppose you would like your car back," was her answer, in her soft, deep voice.

"That and a few other items very dear to me," I answered. I had already decided not to make her wake up on the wrong side of the lawn. She was just too darn beautiful to hurt. I just wanted my car, wallet, dad's knife, and my gold coins back. How she got out of Marathon from here was not my problem. She'll probably be driving someone else's classic car before dark.

"Everything's up in the room." She said and unfolded her body gracefully from the bar stool like a leopard. I paid for both drinks and followed her back to Hyatt Place and up to her room. Once inside, she reached for a medium-sized leather satchel that was sitting on the bed and tossed it across the room toward me.

"It's all in there," she said. I sat on the edge of the bed, unzipped the bag, and peered inside. My Firebird keys sat on top, along with the gold bezel-wrapped Spanish doubloon, the wallet, and my other loose coins. Below that there was a pile of watches, bracelets, necklaces jewels, rings, and several silver and gold antique Spanish coins.

"My, my," I said. "You've been a busy lady. Now I know how you spent your evenings."

"A girl's gotta get by." She responded, without any emotion, or even looking up.

I was busy rummaging through the bag and I almost didn't see the flash of green toenail paint heading for my temple. It was meant to kill or at least disable, but I had training. My head wasn't there. I tossed the satchel aside and stood up. Judy was in fight mode, and she came at me again, not waiting till I got myself in a defensive position. I parried her attack with my forearms. The gentleman in me hesitated, and all I did for the first few moments was defend myself. I can usually make short work of any four drunks in a bar fight, and hold my own against someone professionally trained, but it became obvious all she was planning to do was step across my lifeless body on her way out the door. I don't know where she was trained, but she was nearly a match.

Nearly.

We spared for a minute, neither able to inflict serious damage on each other. That was rare. Real martial arts fights between experts rarely last more than a few seconds before someone is disabled or worse yet, dead. I was quicker and a little more skilled. She was taller with a better reach. But in this type of fight, there's no such thing as a draw. We hand-spared for a little bit before I finally landed a spin-kick to her right side, pinning her arm against her. She let out an "oof!" and retreated, holding her arm. I relaxed and stepped into the bathroom to grab a towel and wipe the sweat out of my eyes,

"You ready to cry 'uncle'?" I asked as I walked out, my face buried in the towel.

That was the last thing I remember.

Flashback - Treachery

Albert Sawyer returned to his wagon and removed the tops of two wooden kegs marked "Nails." Dumping out the contents onto the floor of the wagon, he placed three of the plated bars in the kegs. Then he covered the bars with a burlap sack, and re-filled the kegs with the iron construction nails, hammering the tops shut. As dawn neared, he drove the team down to the Savannah docks, where the *St. Augustine*, a union-flagged, former Confederate blockade runner rested. Supplies and freight were being hauled aboard as he arrived. "Here's the order of nails for my uncle in Key West," he advised the dock master. He provided a bill of lading, and, again a few gold coins changed hands to ensure nobody would question the surprisingly heavy kegs. As planned, a boy from the livery stable showed up to take the team and wagon away, and Sawyer walked up the gangplank, paid the captain steerage fare then moved below to clear a personal spot in the cargo deck for the nine-day trip. If all went as planned, he would return to that barn in a few months and recover all the silver.

The ship sailed under steam with the tide, heading for Key West with planned stops in St. Augustine and Nassau. A large steam-driven side-wheel and two sailing masts powered the *St. Augustine.* Grossing 474 tons, the iron-sided steamship had been an active Confederate Blockade runner from the beginning of the war, running cotton out of Mobile to Havana until she was captured by Union ships in 1863 when she was re-flagged as a Union vessel and used to patrol the Atlantic coast. With the war over, the ship had been sold to the Georgia East Coast Shipping Company and now hauled small freight throughout the Caribbean. Dry goods and cotton to Nassau, rum from Nassau and dry goods to St. Augustine, flour, beans, other foodstuffs and building supplies to Key West, cattle from Key West to Punta Rasa, near the mouth of the Caloosahatchee River by Sanibel Island, then back to Key West for a load of sponges and turtles to take back to Savannah for transfer to New York. The war had interrupted most of this commerce and the industrial north was in need of products and raw materials.

Nine days later, the *St. Augustine* pulled into Mallory Docks in Key West shortly before sunset. While unloading the cargo usually waited till morning, Sawyer was met at the dock with a wagon, and again with some money changing hands, the two nail kegs were offloaded in the twilight and driven to a barn just off Caroline Street.

Sawyer knew his uncle Broderick Sawyer had too much money, and too much greed to pass up what he thought was a potentially profitable, if unscrupulous opportunity. Albert Sawyer had no ties to his island home, no qualms about cheating a relative and no plans to ever see Key West again.

He approached his uncle with the parts of his story that fit his needs. "I led a company of soldiers that helped Jefferson Davis and his cabinet make off with millions in gold and silver ahead of the advancing Union Army," he explained. "We hid most of it in Georgia, but I kept six large gold bars, each about fifty pounds, and hid them in two kegs of nails. At twenty dollars per ounce, that's nearly ninety thousand US dollars." Sawyer continued, "If anyone traces the gold to me, I'm a dead man many times over. But you could melt it down, call it Spanish treasure, and get rich."

"And you want how much for this stolen gold?" Broderick asked.

"Just ten thousand Yankee dollars."

The elder Sawyer raised his eyes. "Is it here?"

"Yes, hidden nearby," Albert replied. "I can take you there tonight, but my ship sails early tomorrow, so I need assurance you will buy them if they are as I described, and I will need to be paid in full before I depart. There's a feed scale in the barn, and you're welcome to verify the weight."

"You're my brother's son, God rest his soul," answered the old man. "If I cannot trust you, whom can I trust? What about the rest of the money you have hidden. What's to be done with that?"

"Oh, other people are now responsible for it," replied Albert, offhandedly. "This was my payment for following their orders," he continued. "They knew how difficult these gold bars would be to sell, so they gave me a large reward with an equally large risk."

"I understand. All right, I will meet you at eleven o'clock. Tell me where."

Albert Sawyer gave his uncle directions, suggested he bring a cart or wagon, and they parted for the evening.

In the dark of night, Albert stepped out of the shadows behind a building on Caroline Street and waved down the horse-drawn wagon. Somewhat dismayed that along with the old man, five of his watermen, two with Navy Colt .36 caliber revolvers in their belts, were also along, presumably to help haul the gold-laden nail kegs and provide security. Albert approached the barn and was pleased to see the padlock was still secure. With one of the sailors holding a kerosene lantern, he pulled a large skeleton key out of his pocket and unlocked the ship's padlock. Stepping inside, his heart sank as he saw all at once, the missing boards at the back of the barn and that one of the kegs had been opened, and the nails were strewn over the floor. "We've been robbed!" he turned to his uncle. "There are still three more bars in the other barrel, but three are gone."

"Well, let's look at what's left," the elder Sawyer replied. "I can still pay you half if they are what you have promised."

Albert turned to the remaining barrel. He turned it upside down and using a crowbar, pried it open. The three large bars spilled out, gleaming gold in the lamplight. Sawyer picked one up and showed it to his uncle, then motioned toward the feed scale. "That's not necessary. I trust that you know what they weigh." The old man reached into his satchel and pulled out several bundles of US currency. He divided it in half and handed one portion over to Albert. "I can't say I find this tasteful, but the Confederacy is dead, and better I have this treasure than a bunch of Yankee carpetbaggers. Albert, I trust that you will keep this transaction quiet. Safe trip, and know you have a home any time you happen to be in this town."

Sawyer shoved the bills into his bag and walked away from the group without as much as a wave. The elder Sawyer waited until he was around the corner, and nodded to one of the sailors, who waited a few more moments before disappearing into the dark. Knowing Sawyer would cut over to Front Street and head toward Mallory Docks, the waterman walked straight down Caroline at a brisk pace and turned right at Simonton Street, very close to the Sawyer mansion. It was easy to see Sawyer walking toward the docks, and easier yet to step behind him as he walked by, clubbing him hard on the back of the head with a lead-filled sap, crushing his skull. Sawyer went down in a heap. The waterman quietly picked up Sawyer's satchel and melted back into the darkness.

13
Sucker Punch

I was in the Navy, SEAL boot camp. They brought in a guy for three weeks to teach us hand-to-hand combat and how to kill or disable someone with just your hands and feet. I was expecting some big brute with arms as big as my thighs, but we were introduced to Mister Morimoto, a little Japanese guy who had to be sixty years old. Heck, I already had two years of close combat training; I didn't think this Karate Kid trainer could show me much beyond "wax on, wax off." Nevertheless, for three weeks I went through the motions in class, never paying that much attention. There wasn't much I didn't think I already knew. Then one day Mirimoto showed up in a ghee, barefoot, tied with an ominous-looking black belt with five white cloth stripes sewed to the end.

"Graduation day," he started. "Who would like to be the first person to take the final?" He looked my way. "Ah, Mr. Wahl, let's see how well you have been paying attention. Your grade will be determined by how effectively you can kill me. Please to start. Remove your shoes and outerwear." He bowed deeply. "We may begin."

"Sir," I stammered "I'm not going to kill you."

"Do not call me sir!" He yelled in my face, "I am a Sargent. I work for a living! And kill me you must, for if you don't kill me, I shall kill you!"

He backed off a few steps and dropped into a fighting stance. They didn't call me "kitten" for no reason. Oh, I could fight, disable, and maim with the best of them, but hated hand-to-hand combat. I figured I would have at least a side-arm on me or a knife, and if I got in a sticky position, I could just shoot or stick the baddies, instead of kicking them to death. It looked like Mr. Mirimoto wasn't going to take a rain check. I took off my shirt, pants, and shoes, and faced my teacher in a tee shirt and boxers. I probably had a hundred pounds on him and four inches of reach. I had no plans to kill him. I figured a few good round house kicks and I could fight the fight out of him and walk away with an "A." No need to waste any time. I bowed because it looked cool and waded right in. Ten minutes later I woke up face down, spitting blood and lying next to five of my classmates.

We all received an "F."

He came back a few months later. I sure paid attention that time. Over the years it probably saved my life more than once. I learned later in life that circumstances don't always give you more weapons than your opponent.

Flashback - Key West, Florida, September 1, 1879

Louisa Galarza Sawyer stood up and stepped out of her bath. Wanda, her personal assistant, and a former slave, wrapped her in her robe. The bathwater had been unheated and felt good in the steamy Key West late August afternoon. In the fading light, Louisa peeked out of her upstairs door, confirmed that nobody was in sight, and stepped out onto the balcony of the mansion and sat down in a rocking chair. Broderick's three teenage children by his first marriage were safely away in boarding school in New York, so the mansion was empty, save the maid, her personal assistant, and the cook staff, all black Bahamian. (His first wife, Sarah died suddenly and somewhat suspiciously from accidental food poisoning.) Knowing her husband was still down at the docks and that nobody else was permitted upstairs but her maid, she slipped the robe off her shoulders, let it fall to her waist, and sat back to let the afternoon sun play on her full, honey-colored breasts.

Like many members of Cuban/Spanish royalty, Moorish conquerors from the 14th Century had either intermarried or raped their way through many Spanish families and, although her eyes were a light hazel, her hair was dark and her skin the color of mocha. She was, without question, the most beautiful woman in Key West. Only twenty-nine years old, she was born when her husband, Broderick Sawyer, turned thirty. He met Louisa in Havana some years earlier, the daughter of one of the most influential families in Cuba. Only seventeen back then, Louisa had been involved in a scandal with an older ship's captain, and Sawyer, quite fetched with her beauty, was surprised when the Galarza family was more than happy to marry her off to the older American as damaged goods and send her away to Key West. Sawyer had owned three slaves for many years before and during the Civil War. Wanda, Louisa's maidservant, his horse attendant and carriage driver Pomp, and Pomp's wife Matilda, the housekeeper and head cook. Once slavery was abolished, he offered them all jobs, destroyed the tiny dirt-floored slave quarters, and paid them two dollars a week. With this pay, far more than the going rate, most of them bought little clapboard shacks west of Whitehead Street behind the Baptist Church on Thomas. Key West had a large population of free blacks even pre-Civil War during the slave era. They were mostly from the Bahamas, where the British Empire had abolished slavery in 1833. They migrated to Key West along with their former masters.

The British loyalists, moved to Key West as wreckers when the government mandated that all salvage go through the Key West Customs House. The free blacks settled in a part of town that became known as Bahama Village.

Sawyer's three chattels blurred the line between free and slave. They could come and go as they pleased, even when they were his property, provided they were off duty. They all went to church on Sundays and were permitted to do outside work during off hours and keep their earnings.

Here's a clip from the New York Times in 1862.

Slavery is now here on the island being brought to the test of the late order of the President, and the Quartermaster's department is employing such Negroes as are needed in that department as laborers, nurses for the sick, and for all or any purpose of labor. Those taken who are claimed by disloyal masters are delighted with the change, and others of the same class who are not thus employed are leaving their masters, and seeking labor or employment on their own account. A custom long in vogue here has prepared the Negro for this, as they have been allowed to hire their own time, and make what they could, paying to their master a portion of their earnings. This latter obligation the darkie proposes to ignore for the future, and applications have been made to the military commandant to have punished such Negroes as refuse to pay over their wages or to work for their masters, which have been invariably refused, on the ground that the soldiers of our army are not to be used to compel the rendering of unrequited labor, thus leaving the slaveholder dependent on moral persuasion to sustain the old relationship. How far this will be successful in keeping them to the line of duty which exacts all his labor for master's benefit, whilst the Negro is merely receiving what will keep him in condition to continue the *arrangement, is one phase of the question now about to be solved. There are many Negroes employed here on our Government Works and otherwise, who were purchased simply for the investment of capital by private individuals, adding Negro after Negro out of the proceeds of such labor. This, although done by men who are classed among good Christians, is yet one of the harsh features of slavery, and stamps the operator with a character for unscrupulousness even among slave-owners. The value of slave property is materially affected by the existing state of things, and an able Negro man of middle age was a few days since offered for sale at $200, without meeting a purchaser. This certainly bears with much hardship upon certain families who are dependent upon the wages and sale of their Negroes for their support and the education of their children. Yet it is somewhat difficult to realize that all the wealth of the island does not still remain with us, or that there is any diminution of the power to do or accomplish. The Negro is no more unwilling to labor when the proceeds are expected to enter his own exchequer, than when he knows they will go into master's. The State Legislature of Florida passed an act in the winter of 1860, providing for the exile or enslavement of all free Negroes within its borders. As there are many of that class of laborers here, there was consequent perturbation among them for a short time under the last of secession rule, until the puny efforts to display the rebel flag became hushed like the assassin's retreat, and the glorious Stars and Stripes were given to the breeze by a force to maintain them. Then these people, reassured at once, became quieted, and now remain as they have been for years, an orderly, industrious, law-abiding, and most useful class, many of whom are carpenters, masons, or seamstresses of respectable abilities.*

Sawyer encouraged all three to learn to read and abhorred any kind of physical punishment. That being said, they were definitely considered "the help", and thusly second-class citizens.

Wanda, over two decades Louisa's senior, stepped out on the veranda looking for her boss and scolded her for being nude outdoors. "Miss Louisa, yo bes cover yo self up," she said. "Massa Broderick be home in a moment, an he won't take kindly to you bein undressed like that outside."

Louisa tossed her black mane. "That old *pindeho*," she retorted in a thick Spanish accent. "Why should it matter to him how I dress? He can't even get it up anymore," but she pulled the robe back around her shoulders and covered her breasts.

Then she turned to Wanda. "Are you going into the village tonight? I have a message for Marcus." She lowered her voice, "tell him I need him to come by tomorrow and trim the roses in the backyard."

Wanda shook her head, standing in disgust with her hands on her hips. "Yeah, I knows what roses you wants trimmed and dey ain't in no backyard. Girl, you best not mess around in yo own henhouse. Massa Broderick gonna catch you someday. He will have Marcus killed then beat yo ass close to death."

Louisa stood up and brushed passed Wanda, walking into her bedroom. She let the robe fall on the floor, and she threw herself onto her bed, face down, motioning Wanda to leave.

"Just give Marcus the message," she said. "Let me worry about that old man."

Shaking her head, Wanda picked up the robe and walked out of Louisa's bedroom, closing the door behind her. Louisa got up and locked the door. She had her own bedroom and had no interest in sharing it tonight, or any other night, with the elder Sawyer. She lay back on top of the bedsheets, nude, cooling off in the evening breeze that wafted through the open louvers and dozed off.

14
You Can't Fly Far on One Wing

I woke up face down on the hotel room carpet in the Hyatt. The back of my neck was killing me and I could taste blood in my mouth and maybe a broken tooth. It was déjà vu all over again. Opening my eyes, I could see Judy sitting in a motel chair, a bag of ice resting on her arm. I dragged myself painfully into a sitting position.

"Why are you still here?" I asked.

"You can't get far with a broken arm," she answered.

Checkmate.

I got off the floor and sat on the side of the bed.

"I should call the cops and have you arrested. Grand theft auto, burglary, credit card fraud, assault, and that's just before lunch." I thought for a moment. "But the cops and I don't always get along that well." I stood up and grabbed the valise full of loot. "Come on, let's get you over to Fisherman's Hospital and get that arm looked at. We'll tell them you fell down or something like that. I held up the valise. "We'll deal with this later." I stopped for a moment on the way to the door. "What's your real name, anyway?"

She hesitated. I guessed, correctly she was coming up with a different name. "Oh, Molly will do," she answered. I didn't know if I should believe her. She got up slowly, holding her forearm, and followed me without another word. Tough girl, but a broken bone or two will take the fight out of anyone.

Fisherman's Hospital took our made-up story at face value I told them she had a little too much to drink at the Sunset Grille near the Seven Mile Bridge and took a tumble down the stairs. No, we aren't going to sue. Her dumb fault. No, we didn't have them call an ambulance and pay a grand for a two-mile ride. Three hours and fifteen hundred bucks later we were sprung; broken ulna, cracked radius, and two bruised ribs. She walked out with her arm in a cast and sling, and her ribs wrapped. I paid the bill and we walked out to the parking lot. She reached out with her good hand.

"I guess this is where we say good-bye unless you are going to call the cops."

"Nonsense," I answered. "Get in the car."

"Where are we going?" Molly asked.

"Back to the inn," I answered. "You're going to get better, then wash dishes, dust furniture, and clean windows for, like, the next five hundred years. They say keep your friends close, and your enemies closer. I'm going to wear you like my favorite sweatshirt. Besides, I want to learn how you got my man-cave open, and I would love to learn how you do that nifty backward spin kick."

We rode in silence for at least twenty minutes before she spoke. "Finding your secret room was sort of an accident." She said as we drove south. "I figured out two things a few days after I got there. First off, the outside architecture of the building didn't match the inside design." I must have looked a little surprised. "Yes, I managed to scout the whole place at night when everyone was asleep. It only took a few days to figure out what was missing, and where. After that, I got in your room when you weren't around. Those skeleton keys look nifty but they won't lock out a paraplegic monkey. Once in your front room I poked, prodded, and pulled things until the room opened," she smiled. "Cute. Anne Frank in Hebrew, which I speak fluently. I speak six languages."

"You said you figured out two things. What was the other?" I asked

"You have a huge private hidden room, and keep a two hundred thousand dollar classic car in a garage. Everyone calls you 'boss' even though all you do is cook. You don't just work there. You own it."

Flashback – New Year's Eve 1870

Key West in the 1870's was in many ways much different than today's artsy, liberal-minded community, but if you walked down the streets of Old Town a hundred fifty years ago, much of modern Key West would be recognizable. Grand mansions graced tree-lined streets much as today, but they were private family residences owned by rich merchants and wreckers instead of bars, and guesthouses. Only a few streets were paved, mostly by brick brought from Boston, Chicago, or New York. Side streets were little more than dirt roads.

What we call New Town today was mostly non-existent, with only the salt ponds being built, but not till the 1880's. Before that, the eastern part of the island consisted mostly of marshlands, mangroves, a bay, and the occasional crocodile. Downtown Key West featured many of the same buildings we see today but occupied by dry goods merchants and shipbuilding suppliers instead of tee-shirt shops and souvenir stores. Oh, there was no shortage of bars, even back then and dance clubs were most popular. Always located at the end of horse-drawn street car lines, they entertained huge crowds nearly every weekend.

As he did on most mornings, Broderick Sawyer was up and gone to his office above Tift's warehouse in Mallory Square. The building was built with bricks brought one by one from Chicago to Savannah by train, then by paddlewheel steamship from there to Key West. It was built so solidly it survives to this day and houses the popular *El Meson de Pepe*. The elder Sawyer always left to walk to his office in a white suit and silver-tipped cane, even in the middle of the sweltering summer, usually before Louisa got up. But this morning Wanda was knocking on her door before eight. She raised her voice so she could be heard through the door. "Miss Louisa, you needs to be up. Mista George be comin over dis morning to work on yo portrait." Wanda rattled the door knob. "Git up, missy. I has to dress yo and do yo hair."

Louisa rose, and used the chamber pot located under a wicker chair in the corner. "That green dress is so heavy and hot. Tell the painter to come back in the fall when it cools."

"I'll do no such ting!" yelled Wanda through the door. "Dis be the las day he coming. I hears him tell Massa Sawyer he can finish de res of de portrait wifout you, jes have de dress in his studio." Fifteen years after being given her freedom, Wanda, who was born into slavery, still called the elder Sawyer "Massa" out of habit. Having been a handmaiden to Louisa since the Cuban arrived in Key West before her eighteenth birthday, the headstrong maid treated Mrs. Sawyer with a strong-willed flippant liberty a mother usually reserves for an errant child.

Louisa rose from the chair and unlocked the door. Wanda entered Louisa's bedroom and set a chair in the middle of the room. Still nude, she reluctantly sat in the chair. Wanda approached her with her undergarments and dress. "No undergarments today, Wanda," Louisa instructed. "It's dreadfully hot and I'll be sitting for that portrait for hours downstairs." Wanda shrugged and slipped the green silk dress over Louisa's nude body. Taking a hairbrush and comb, she brushed her jet black hair back, and slid a large tortoise-shell comb into the top of her hair. Applying rouge and lip color, she finished the ensemble by opening a jewelry box on the dressing table and slipping the large gold, jewel-encrusted cross around her neck, avoiding the piled-high hairdo. "Do I have to wear this disgusting thing?" she asked. "The painter finished that part last month. It's too heavy."

"Yes, Missy, you do," replied Wanda. "The artist be downstairs waiting and he minded me that you gots to be wearin it. He still have some more work to do." Wanda continued. "Besides, it's yo father's mos treasured heirloom in your fambily. The Galarza family's had it for generations, and it be passed down to you for safekeeping." Wanda added softly, "today's your las setting." Wanda reminded Louisa again, redundantly. "The artist say he can complete the rest of the portrait wifout you."

"Finally," Louisa answered. "It's been months. I would have never agreed to this if Broderick had commissioned it, but this portrait was ordered by my father and I can never say no to him. He's been such a good father and now he grows old. His time comes near."

Dressing completed, *sans cullotes,* Louisa rose and strode down the steps barefoot to the awaiting portrait artist. It was warm, but she chose to not wear any undergarments for a different reason than comfort. She sat down and the artist, using his unfinished work as a guide, positioned the woman correctly; chin high, eyes forward as if looking directly at the admirer. "This is the last sitting today, Mrs. Sawyer," the artist commented. "Hold still for just a while longer and I can finish the portrait in my studio without you." She nodded, bored, and glanced outside through the big bay window toward the garden. Her heart raced a little when she saw the gardener, Marcus, his sweat glistening jet black muscles rippling on his bare chest, was trimming palm fronds back by the carriage barn. She wanted to run outside now into his arms but dared not. At least this portrait was nearly complete. She sat still, trying not to fidget. After two hours, the artist looked up. "Done, Mrs. Sawyer, I can finish the work in my studio now. I will bring the finished portrait to you in six weeks. Thank you for your patience. I believe you will like my work."

"I don't really care about your work," she snapped, tossing her head. "It will be shipped to Cuba when it's done and will find a place to gather dust over some fireplace in my father's mansion."

The artist bowed in polite understanding, and Louisa flashed out the door into the backyard. She pretended to inspect the mangos for ripeness, taking her time until she caught the attention of the gardener, Marcus. After a brief moment of eye contact and a tiny nod, she casually walked into the carriage barn and waited. A few moments later Marcus softly came in through the side door. Rushing into his sweat-covered torso, she kissed him fiercely without a word and buried her face in his musky odor. "Where Massa Sawyer?" Marcus asked quietly.

"In his office on Tift Alley," she answered. "We won't see him for hours."

Marcus knew well what he was there for. Forcefully, he spun Louisa around and pushed her head down over the carriage. Untying the twine that held his trousers up, he stepped out of them over his calloused bare feet. Immediately erect, he boosted Louisa's dress up around her waist and with animal roughness, entered her. She gasped, always surprised at his hugeness. He thrust several times, and with a groan, spent himself inside her. They remained thusly for a minute, both enjoying the afterglow.

Suddenly, the carriage door opened, and, in the doorway backlit by the afternoon sun, stood the elderly Broderick Sawyer. "Scoundrel!" he roared, reaching inside his coat, he produced a two-shot thirty-two caliber Derringer. Marcus was already moving. Gathering up his pants, he raced for the side door. A shot rang out and wood splintered above the black man's head. A second shot filled the room with smoke and noise. The black man screamed and grabbed at his shoulder, before reaching the side door of the carriage barn. Bursting through the door, still naked and trailing blood, he dashed down the side yard and out of sight. "I'll deal with him shortly.

Turning to his wife, he yelled. "Like that darkie, do you? I'll teach you a lesson, you ungrateful bitch!" Frozen in fear, with her dress still up around her waist, her fist to her mouth, Louisa stood in the middle of the barn.

The old man looked around the room for something to punish the woman with. Seeing only a military camp shovel, he impulsively picked it up and with one swing, nearly severed her head. In anger, he swung the shovel several times more at the limp body, huddled lifeless on the dirt floor. He took the head entirely off and then finished with several blows to her torso. The side door opened again and Wanda stood there and began to scream. "Caught her with that gardener, Marcus," Sawyer heaved, breathing hard. "Go get the Key West police over here. This was justified." The old man reached down to the ground and picked up the bloody golden cross where it lay after falling to the ground from her severed neck. "This is mine!" he exclaimed. "She doesn't need it now."

IOANNES.V.D.G.PORT.ET.ALG.REX

15
DWB – Dishwasher with Benefits

We got back to Key West in an hour and I parked the Firebird back in the garage. We walked inside and I asked Scarlet for the key to 102 and she handed it over with a disdainful dirty look, too smart to comment. My gang's smarter than to ask questions they don't need to know what happened, but they couldn't help but notice the cast on her arm and the shiner that was growing under my left eye. We walked silently down the hall toward the room. When we were out of earshot, I turned.

"Here." I said, quietly handing the key over. "I'll keep this bag of loot and figure out a way to get it back to the cops. I assume it's all local booty?"

"All but one coin I brought with me," she said. She took the valise from me and dug into the bottom. Pulling out a large gold coin in a hard plastic holder, she handed it over.

"This is what got me to come down and hide. I snag one little gold coin and half the Kansas City mob puts out a contract on me."

I took the plastic holder and examined the coin. You could read the date, 1787. A goofy-looking eagle on one side and a sort of rising sun on the other. The initials EB were stamped next to the eagle. Suddenly I realized I was looking at something I had only read about and seen pictures of in books. My eyes got wide.

"Is this real?" I asked. "Do you know what it is?"

"It's some kind of a gold coin," she answered. "I cracked a pretty good safe in a mob boss' house, so I have to assume it's not fake. I was able to grab a bunch of cash and about a half million in bearer bonds and this coin, but I hear they didn't seem to care much about the cash and the bonds, only the coin. What's the big deal?"

"If it's what I think it is, it's the rarest coin in the world. From what I've read, they only know of seven Brasher Doubloons in existence. This makes eight."

"What's so important about it?"

I looked at the ceiling to recall. "Ephraim Brasher was a

silversmith who lived next door to George Washington in New York City following the Revolutionary War. He made lots of coins, and all of them are pretty valuable now, but he made just a few gold doubloons. They got famous after a book was written about one being stolen, and I think they made a movie back in the forties. The last one sold for over five million dollars. I can bet they are pissed that you stole it."

She gave a low whistle. "Leave it up to me to steal something really valuable. Is there any way to get them off my ass?"

"Let me make some calls," I answered. "I have a friend who knows people that know people. Maybe I can convince the baddies to go away. In the meantime, I suggest you go back into that Mother Hubbard disguise you fooled me with before. It wouldn't be smart that word got out a six-foot-tall plus-ten fox was hanging out around my pool."

I took the valise along with the Brasher Doubloon and put them safely (except for Molly) in my room. Taking my own personal items out, I tore off the leather handles to make sure there was nothing that might hold fingerprints. Molly has assured me she wore gloves during all of her heists. I called over Bela and handed him the bag.

"Take this down to Fleming Street and stuff it behind the dumpster behind Faustos Grocery Store. Cover it with some newspaper, then come right back and let me know when it's done." He nodded without a word and headed down the alley behind the inn. He returned ten minutes later. "All done, boss. I didn't even look inside." I could tell by his flushed face he did look inside, but I was also certain he would never have touched any of the loot.

After dark, I snuck out of the inn over to Duval Street. Just south of Truman is one of the few payphones left in downtown Key West. I dialed 9-1-1, figuring it was the quickest way to cut the red tape.

"9-1-1 what is your emergency?" a disinterested voice asked. I'm sure she had spent the whole shift answering drunk, disorderly, bicycle thefts, stolen dildos, and domestic violence calls.

I skipped the pleasantries. "When I hang up, go talk personally to Johnny Russell. Tell him to check behind the dumpster at Faustos for a prize. He will know what to do." And I hung up before someone rolled on the location that had been instantly identified by the 9-1-1 call. I would be back home before a patrol car came by the pay phone or Johnny got to Faustos. I recommended Johnny for two reasons; one, he was an honest cop, and two; I wanted my cousin to get the brownie points for recovering stolen merchandise from a dozen burglaries.

The next night Molly showed up at happy hour for the first time, feeling comfortable since there were no other guests around. With no Yukon Jack on the menu, she settled for a beer. I decided to break the ice.

"Where the hell did you learn to fight like that?"

"Subic Bay, Philippines." She answered, languidly stretching out on a lounge, her long legs crossed. "Navy brat. Dad was on base all day and I was left alone. I was twelve years old when we got there from Valdosta, Georgia. On the first day I went outside the base, I was attacked four times. The fourth time I was gang-raped by six guys and left naked in an alley. I was too embarrassed to tell dad and have him turn it into a federal incident. A few weeks after that I started looking for a martial arts academy. It took me five tries, but I finally found one that agreed to teach a skinny little white girl. I learned how to fight, and quick. A few months later I found those boys. Needless to say, they won't rape any more helpless girls. Word got out around town and nobody bothered me after that."

I rubbed the back of my neck. "After I woke up, I figured you would be long gone. Why did you hang around?"

"Two reasons." She answered, softly. "One, I had a broken arm and needed help. I suspected the real you had a soft side. And two, the same as your question. Where did you learn to fight? I've fought three men at once in the past and they never laid a hand on me. You were beating the hell out of me."

"Oh, I got some training in the Navy," I answered, somewhat vaguely.

"I'll call bullshit on that answer," she retorted. "I've fought my share of sailors. And most sailors can't fight their way out of a wet paper bag. I need a better answer than that. Navy? It had to be an elite combat unit. You must have been a Seal."

I gulped and didn't say a word either way.

The next day I called my old buddy, Bo Morgan, one of the few people besides Rumpy and the kids who knew "Bric" was still alive. Bo had sold the houseboat and the boat *Captain Morgan* and was living in Palm Bay now with his son, Tack. I told him I had a hot Brasher Doubloon, and how I got it.

Bo whistled slowly at the words 'Brasher Doubloon'. "That's gonna be harder to get rid of than throwing a piece of tape. Let me make some calls and see if I can figure out a way to get people to play nice." There was a moment's hesitation. "Does this girl mean anything to you? She might still run afoul of my acquaintances even if she returns the merchandise. It's just the way they roll. They aren't that big at forgiving. I will remind you of the famous or infamous people throughout history who have just vanished without a trace. Almost all of them had done a 'favor', and were 'forgiven'."

"She doesn't really mean a thing," I answered. "She stole my car and some of my stuff, and I got it back so no harm no foul. I guess I wanted to give her a break and pay it forward a bit."

"She must be a looker. Sounds like you're thinking with the little head again. You know what that's got you in the past."

I grinned sheepishly to myself. "Don't remind me," I answered. "I haven't got in her nickers even once." I hesitated for a moment, "though I wouldn't turn it down."

"That's what I thought," said Bo. "I was pretty sure female body parts had something to do with it." He gave out a deep sigh. "Let me call some friends and see if we can get this fixed. Can she borrow your car and bring me the coin?"

"She's 'borrowed' it enough," I answered, smiling to myself. "I'll bring her and the Brasher to you."

Bo called a few weeks later with the news. He reached a go-between who assured him she could bring him the Brasher Doubloon so he could give it back and there would be no hard feelings. That night I gave Molly the plan. I would drive her up to Ft Lauderdale and we would play tourist for a few days. On Saturday, we would meet at Bo's place and hand over the coin, then take our time coming home. She nodded agreement and we loaded a few belongings into the Firebird.

"You planning on coming back?" I asked.

"Yes, she answered quietly. I'm tired of running. I'll come back and wash your dishes for a while. Maybe I can eventually find a life down here."

That night I decided to use my man-cave so I could stretch out in peace. I gunned a few vodka cranberries and then crawled into my king-size bed. Maybe an hour later, I heard my secret bookcase slowly open with a creak. I feigned sleep but braced for an attack. If they had a gun, I was dead anyway. Then I heard the rustle of clothes falling to the floor and then felt the hardness of a plaster cast. She spoke quietly.

"You said to keep your enemies closer. Thought I'd see how close I could get."

I reached for Molly and felt for her lips with mine. That first kiss was as nice as I thought it would be.

16
A Badly Needed Break

The trip north, taken late at night, less my car was recognized, was quiet, but full of smiles. For the first time in a few years, I was falling in love again. She was so different than anyone before, beautiful and mysterious. We both had lives to leave behind, mine to move on from and hers to forget.

We checked into the Riverside Hotel, a quaint, old place in the middle of downtown Lauderdale, and we turned tourists. The following morning, we went south to Haulover Beach, one of the only recognized nude beaches in Florida and we left our worries behind us when we threw our clothes on the sand. After a morning of sun and snorkeling in the buff, we found a Cuban restaurant and munched tasty Cuban sandwiches, a mixture of ham and pork, topped with spicy mustard and a pickle on Cuban bread toasted Panini style. Being a hundred and fifty miles north of the rock, I didn't need a disguise and could enjoy life in public for the first time in months. We went back to Las Olas Boulevard and bar-hopped the tree-lined street till late in the evening, two people in love and lust, knowing the night would end in ecstasy.

We returned to the room around two and started throwing our clothes off well before we got to the room. Boy, was that housekeeper surprised when the elevator opened to serious half-naked foreplay! Outside of more than one *cuba libre,* I staggered to the door and put the key in. We wasted little time finishing getting undressed, and I jumped on the four poster bed. Spread eagled and ready. Slyly, Molly reached in her bag and pulled out a length of rope. "I took the liberty of borrowing this from your gardener before we left," she said. Molly crawled on top of my chest and straddled me, wearing nothing but black thong panties. "Want to have a little fun?" She looped one end around my left wrist. "First, me. I'll have my way with you. And then it's your turn." I nodded agreement, too drunk to argue. I didn't care who did what to whom, as long as we did it.

Expertly, she tied both hands to the posts, and then climbing off me, she tied both feet, spread wide, to each side of the antique four-poster bed. Tied hand and foot, she slid off her panties, and crammed them completely in my mouth, then secured them by slipping the leg of another pair of underwear over my head and lips. Hot damn! This was gonna be fun! What came next was a complete surprise; she bent over and kissed me on the forehead. "I'll put the 'do not disturb' sign on the door," she said, wriggling into her shorts and tank top. "If you can't get out of the knots, which I doubt, they should open the room by tomorrow afternoon. By then, I'll be long gone, so don't even come looking. Don't worry; I won't take your precious car. It's a little too obvious anyway. You'll find it in the parking lot, where you left it. Oh, you won't get home that easy. I'll have your keys, so you can't hurry off. I'm sorry Bric, but a girl's gotta do what a girl's gotta do. Yes, I know who you are, I found out the day I got there. You need to find a better place to hide papers."

And with that, she kissed my forehead again and, flicked my quickly un-erecting dick with her index finger. Blowing me a kiss she whirled and walked out.

I'll be dammed.

It took four hours to get the panties out of my mouth, earing a very sore tongue in the process, not in the fashion I had planned. I started hollering and the manager on duty finally responded, blushing bright red when she entered the room. She nodded knowingly. I tried to explain. "It isn't what it looks like, well not exactly. Please untie me."

First throwing a bath towel over the privates, she fiddled with the knots for twenty minutes before calling housekeeping, then a bellman. By then I had a bigger crowd in my room than the dancing extras that instantly show up in an Elvis movie. Nobody had a pocket knife. After half the hotel made the attempt, I was about out of patience. I was turning out to be the *Entertainment Du Jour* for the Riverside Hotel. They finally gave up and called the paramedics. They showed up a few minutes later with ominous-looking equipment and enough staff to storm Omaha Beach. "No Jaws of

Life," I cautioned.

Then the six o'clock news, who heard the call over the fire radio showed up.

Sheesh.

After an hour with sharp things near places where they shouldn't oughta be, I was freed. Excusing everyone, I retreated into the bathroom to dress. Fortunately, she took my keys but left my shorts and wallet, less any loose cash. Properly attired, I was no longer an attraction, and everyone left. I grabbed my bag and checked out. Just like Molly said, the Firebird was downstairs, sitting safely where I had left it the night before. I walked up to the car, and reaching under the left front fender, pulled out the Hide-A-Key.

Momma didn't raise no fool.

I took the phone out of the glovebox and called Bo. "No sign of her" came the craggy voice.

"I didn't think so, but it was worth the try. Let your buddies know I got hoodwinked too." I sighed heavily. "By now there's no telling where she is. She might have gone to the airport this morning and will be sunning someplace nekid on Saint Somewhere by the afternoon."

"My acquaintances won't be very happy about this," Bo answered slowly.

"Explain to them this wasn't any of my doing. I was as caught off guard as they were."

"They tend not to care much for excuses," Bo answered. "They're not even that good with legitimate stories. I'll tell them what happened but it might not be taken well."

My next call was to the inn. Scarlet answered. "Nobody's Inn Key West," she said. "Will the last one out of town turn out the lights?"

"Scarlet it's me," I answered. "I'll be home tonight. We got dry-gulched."

"What you mean 'we' Batman? You got a mouse in yo pocket? I didn't trust her from the day she got back. But I wasn't the one who wanted to slip the banana into the Chiquita."

I ignored the remark and gave her the Readers Digest version of the day's fun and games.

"That explains a few things. Some people be calling you, and de Channel Six News called askin' if the breakfast cook be back yet. Dey wants a statement."

"It figures. If the news calls again tell them I joined the French Foreign Legion. If anyone else calls, I'll be back late tonight and will be happy to chat. People with bent noses with last names ending in vowels think I'm in on some of their missing merchandise that our former guest took."

I cruised around Fort Lauderdale and Miami for a few hours, just on the wild chance Molly hung around. By dark, I was pretty sure she wasn't going to be seen on a street corner with her thumb out. Reluctantly, I headed back down the keys, stopping at Alabama Jacks for a beer and a combo basket. It just didn't taste as good while I ate, expecting an Italian *lupara* shotgun round through my back at any moment, al a Luca Brasi in the *Godfather*.

I got back to Key West later that night. I was surprised to see Rumpy sitting in the lobby, fortifying himself with an extra-large boat drink.

"Give Bo a call." He said with an ashen face. I tapped his number on my cell phone. Bo answered, and I could tell it wasn't his best day. "I guess she never planned to bring me the Brasher, and decided to set up shop on South Beach for a while. Normally that kind of news results in a death sentence for me but they know if I ended up under the lawn, I would be able to reach out from the grave. Anyway, they were able to track her down. News reported they found a girl on South Beach last night. Tall redhead, nude to the waist in torn cutoffs. They described it as an apparent mob hit. Double tap to the forehead. No identification. I think it's your girl."

I was speechless. Another woman dead because she got involved with me. Not that she wouldn't have probably run afoul of bad guys sooner or later.

"There's more. The guys that were most likely the murderers, dropped by the house tonight. My address was on a piece of paper in her bag, as was yours. Since I'm a friend of friends, they know I had nothing to do with the theft. I told them you were cool too, but I don't know for sure that will stick, I suggest you watch your back."

I guess I'm too hardened to grieve much. I was mad at her for pulling the wool over my eyes and a little bit satisfied she got what was coming to her, and I was mad at myself for letting her get to me. She seemed so sincere after I broke her arm.

Now, if Bo was right, she might have caught me up in something that I had only been trying to fix. For several days, I scrutinized every check-in, but all were innocent couples, single gay men, and girlfriend getaways. Then one afternoon we got a visitor that didn't fit. Surprisingly, a woman, looking uncomfortable in tourist garb. No reservation and paid cash. Just something about her that gave me the chills. I spent the next three nights in my man cave, with my nine-millimeter glock under my pillow. I stuffed four pillows under the covers in my "real" room; to look like I was still in there, sound asleep, but nobody came.

Two nights later my suspect showed up at my "happy hour." She caught me sort of with my pants down, unarmed with my Glock far away from me upstairs. Anyway, with a pair of swim shorts and a tee shirt, there wouldn't be a place to hide the heat anyway. After looking her over I was more at ease. She wasn't much more heavily dressed than I was; her legs and arms were snow white; the worst Chicago winter tan I'd ever seen. Hell, I didn't even know if she *was* my suspected hit man, er, woman. She ordered scotch/rocks and waited till all the other guests had wandered off. When we were alone, she spoke. I jumped about three feet in the air.

"Some people I work for sent me down here to chat with you," she started. "I must say, there are worse assignments. Nice place." I didn't answer, but poured a drink with slightly shaky hands and sat down in the chair across from her. I figured if she was gonna kill me, I'd already be dead.

She went on. "My associates recently recovered some merchandise in Miami that belonged to us. We're concerned you had something to do with it not being returned as promised. A mutual acquaintance tells us you had nothing to do with it not being returned, and you were misled too." She sipped her drink, letting the ice cubes rattle around the empty glass. I jumped up and offered a refill. She waived me off. I sat back down and went on to tell her what happened in the hotel. "You can check the papers from a few days ago," I offered. "I was trying to help her return the merchandise. I had no idea I was being misled."

"We value the word of our mutual acquaintance. I just wanted to drop by and let you know there's nothing to worry about.

Anyway, I got the chance to enjoy a little vacation. I'll be leaving tomorrow," she stood up and held her hand out. "Good night, Mr. Phillips. Thank you for your charming hospitality."

And with that, she took the back stairs up to her room.

I would have felt more at ease if she had run into a crowded theater and yelled "fire!"

She left the next morning, paying cash and leaving no forwarding address.

Goodbye, Ms. Smith.

Flashback – Later That Day

The local authorities came to the house in just a few minutes time. After hearing Sawyer's explanation that his wife had been caught in a compromising position with a black man, they exonerated him on the spot. That evening, the Key West police canvased Bahama Village for Marcus. The story of the incident had already spread throughout the village, and everyone knew well that Marcus would be tried and executed on the spot. To protect themselves, they knew better than to deny his existence or whereabouts. "He done left dis rock," his mother exclaimed.

With little regard for privacy and procedure in the black community, the police went house to house looking for their suspect, but the wounded man was safely hiding in an attic, and would later be spirited off the island to relatives in the Bahamas by sympathetic relatives. It would be more than a hundred years before any of his descendants would return to Key West. By then, interracial relationships were not only legal but common. The search party was unable to find Marcus but their search did discover his half-brother. Later that evening, the local police, with the assistance of the Key West Klu Klux Klan, took him into custody and hung him from a banyan tree.

Broderick Sawyer never remarried after Louisa's murder. He merely sent word back to Havana that she had died, hoping the Cuban family would never find out how. They sent word asking for the cross to be returned, but he never answered, and after the elder Galarza passed, the significance and history of the cross died with him. After Sawyer's death, the mansion continued to house various members of the family, surviving on the vast riches and business investments amassed by Broderick.

After the old man passed, his children took over the residence and the house was awake and lively for generations with the sounds of laughing children, and delightful smells every day from the cook shed. Both children and adults constantly ran into the ephemeral house guests, but they always seemed harmless and were always welcome, almost as playmates. They delighted especially during windy fall nights, when they appeared more often, to the delight of the Sawyer children, who always invited friends over for slumber parties. Families moved on and away and upkeep and renovations fairly ceased by the turn of the century. The house saw the coming of Henry Flagler's railroad, survived prohibition and the depression, the Spanish-American War, and two world wars.

During the Second World War, with just Mrs. Sawyer occupying the mansion, the Army commandeered the house, as an officer's billet, but changed locations after a few weeks after pestering by the mansion's invisible residents. kitchen, laundry facilities, and shared use of the single bathroom.

Broderick's great-granddaughter became the final matriarch of the family, ruling the household until her death at the age of ninety-one. Surrounded by her immediate family, and all three spirits, she crossed over and was escorted by her ephemeral residents to the golden passageway and a peaceful eternity. Her hosts and longtime houseguests, however, were only able to point the way and could not follow.

17
One Year Later

It had been a year since the hurricane. Key West was back to its old self, having received only a glancing blow. Oh, there were old haunts that had been closed down, bars and restaurants that had been hanging on by their fingernails, failing due to minor damage they couldn't afford to repair, a lack of customers, a shortage of help, or a combination thereof.

The mainstays, including Sloppy Joes, Hogs Breath, Schooner Wharf, the 801, Green Parrot, B.O.'s Fishwagon, and the Hogfish, survived.

There were also more than the usual crops of new names, and establishments, all opened by people with a big bank account and little bookkeeping sense, convinced that two plus two equals five. Those storefronts will probably be vacant again just as soon as the checkbook won't balance.

Aside from a few tree branches that should have been thinned anyway, Nobody's Inn was completely intact. The same didn't apply to businesses and homes from Cudjoe Key to Marathon. The damage to houses and lives was devastating. Business slowly got back toward normal, but I'm not sure that area will fully recover in my lifetime. Reality hits when you see a sofa bed still stuck nine feet up a pine tree a year after the storm, but life goes on and the keys survive.

I got up extra early this morning. For one thing, one of my guests had invited me to go fishing. Another, it was the only holiday, other than Halloween and Christmas that I really celebrated. It also just happened to be my birthday, but I stopped celebrating those when I was about fifty-five. Karen used to ask me every year what I wanted for my birthday and my standard answer was always "a three-way" which always resulted in a disgusting look and a poorly aimed kick toward the balls. I could always avoid the kick bur I hated the dirty look. After a few failed requests, she stopped asking and I stopped suggesting. No biggie. I wasn't going to get my wish anyway. I didn't need a tie or a pair of socks, so I just stopped celebrating birthdays. Besides September six marks a much more significant event and I could celebrate that in lieu of my birthday.

My guests stumbled downstairs at the crack of five; first Lana then her wife just a minute behind. Lana was a shortish blonde with spikey hair and dirty blue jeans. Cindy was a plus-eight classic GLM (good-looking momma) five ten, one fifty, with a short bob of slightly greying brown hair, and a permanent smile. Her choice of morning attire, just silk boxers, and a tank top complimented the package. If she was down here by herself, and straight, or at least bi, she would be both approachable and approached.

"Coffee – black and lots of it. Pour two cups," mumbled Lana in a masculine voice. I was able to tell from the time they checked in who literally wore the pants in the family. "Do you have an IV bag so I can mainline this caffeine?" asked her wife. Lana and Cindy had been crawling the south end of Duvall all night, taking advantage of Women's Fest, participating in the foam dance at Bourbon Street Pub till who knows when. Uncle Eddie 'woofed' their arrival only about an hour before I got up. I sat both mugs on the table. "You'll have to settle for good old-fashioned cups," I answered.

"Breakfast?" I asked. Lana answered for both of them. "Eggs, scrambled with lots of greasy bacon to soak up some of this alcohol. Rye toast with lots of butter. And keep this coffee coming." I turned to my stove, got things cooking, and multi-tasked, putting the icing and candles on my cake. "What's the special occasion?" Cindy asked. "Someone's birthday?"

I was waiting for an opening to launch my tale and they were the only guests in-house. "Oh, much more important," I answered. "Eat your eggs, while I tell you a story." I lapsed into my best television documentary voice.

"About four hundred and fifty years ago, when the 1622 Treasure fleet left Spain in April, it carried wine, cloth, ironwork, and books to distribute to Spanish settlements in the Americas. It also carried around half a million pounds of mercury, which would be used to extract silver from ore mined in what is now Bolivia. When the fleet reached the New World, the ships began trading their goods for the riches of the Americas. They took on silver from Peru, gold bars and silver coins from New Granada, tobacco, indigo, and tons of Cuban copper.

Fleet officials were already getting nervous; hurricane season had started. The oppressive tropical summer heat was intense, and workers cursed and sweated in the baking sun as they loaded cargo and tended their ships. The Atocha and its sister vessels remained docked at Havana while their captains awaited the new moon, which they believed would provide fairer sailing weather until they could get past the dangerous Florida coast. On September 4th, the fleet finally put out to sea.

Less than two days later, a powerful hurricane passed over the fleet near the Dry Tortugas, snapping masts and scattering the ships. Two of the ships, Nuestra Señora de Atocha and the Santa Margarita, sunk within sight of one another after running aground between Key West and the Dry Tortugas. Only five people from the Atocha survived: one sailor, two ship's boys, and two slaves.

The loss of the treasure of the Atocha and the Santa Margarita was a significant financial blow for Spain. The Spanish Government needed this money to run the country, especially the military, which was involved at this time in the ongoing Thirty Years' War plaguing Central Europe. The Spanish sent salvage ships to the supposed site of the wreck, where indigenous slaves dove to the sea floor with the aid of a diving bell to search for the lost cargo. Eventually, the Spanish recovered about half of the treasure lost from the Santa Margarita. One Spanish recovery mission found the location of the Atocha, but the water was too deep for divers to reach it. The Spaniards had little choice but to abandon the wreck and its treasure in the churning waters of the Florida Straits, where it would remain for over 300 years."

The couple was badly hung over, but breakfast was starting to bring them into focus. "Go on," Lana urged. "You sure seem to know about this. Where did you learn so much?"

I didn't dare to tell them I used to be a treasure diver and tried to find that wreck for half a dozen years. "Uh, I read a lot," I stumbled with an answer. "Aw, everyone on this rock knows that story. Just some know about it a little better than others."

"You haven't told us the significance of the cake," Cindy said.

"Because the *Atocha* and the *Santa Margarita* sunk on this day, September 6th," I answered. "What better reason than to celebrate one of the richest shipwrecks in history? Mel Fisher and company salvaged over four hundred million worth of silver, a little gold, and a bunch of emeralds. They still pull treasure from those ships today."

"How wonderful it would be to dive for treasure," Lana remarked. Turning to me, she asked, "don't you wish you could dive one day and find millions?"

"Not me," I answered. " I can't even snorkel without choking on water. I'm happy to stay here and cook breakfast every morning for nice people like you. Leave the adventures to the adventurous."

Looking at her watch, Lana rose. "Speaking of adventure, Captain Bill said six forty-five. We better skedaddle." I grabbed my hat and a pre-made cooler stocked with dolphin wraps for lunch. "Don't you need a hat?" I asked Cindy. She reached for her beach bag. "No hat. I'm out there for sun, not fish. You guys catch dinner, I'll catch some rays. It's the first time in a boat without the kids in years. Four adopted children back home in San Diego, all with severe disabilities. It's a twenty-four-hour, seven-day responsibility." She thought for a second and then frowned. "I hope you aren't too shy or get embarrassed too easily because I plan to get an *even* tan today. It's my one chance this year to blur these tan lines."

I smiled my best "aw shucks" smile. "Ma'am, I've been called a lot of things in my life, but 'shy' or 'embarrassed' aren't two of them." She didn't answer but extended her arm with a 'thumbs up' signal on the way to the car.

We got to the marina and pulled up behind an all too familiar boat. Oh shit, I thought. *That* Captain Bill. He would know the real "me" all too well from the countless fishing trips I used to bum off him years ago. Should I feign a sudden fear of the sea and run for cover? Hell Bric, you want to live in fear forever? I decided to chance it, pulled my Costas on even though it was barely sunrise, and pulled my hat down low. I got introduced to someone I knew all too well and knew me. Fortunately, the deck hand was young enough to have been in diapers when the real 'me' died, so there was no reason to hide as long as I stayed towards the back of the boat.

We cruised out into Florida Straits past the water change where the water from the reef mixed with the Gulf Stream. We idled down to a slow troll amid glassy calm water, just a few yards from the choppy eddy. Cindy kept her promise, stepping up to the long bow of the cruiser. After spreading out a towel, she boldly peeled off her tank top. Out of the corner of my eyes, I caught a glimpse of a beautiful pair of knockers with erect brown nipples through the boat's Plexiglas windshield. If Bill was paying attention, he was doing a good job of ignoring her, as he peered intently into the distance, scouting for water birds. The mate, on the other hand, was having trouble with her modesty, or rather lack thereof, and tripped over the chum bucket before almost doing a face plant over the dual fighting chairs, nearly tripping over the side. "Careful there cowboy," Lana cautioned. "Why don't you stop for a moment and get a good look at her, then go back to being a professional deck hand, before you fall over something else and impale me with that Bubba knife you're cutting bait with." Lana motioned toward the bow. "Go ahead. She won't mind." Cindy, aware of the commotion, chose that instant to slide out of the silk boxers, leaving nothing but a tiny black thong bottom. She hesitated for a moment and peeled them down her legs too. She stretched the elastic and shot them off her index finger toward the mate, who dived out of the way like it was was a flaming arrow. She laughed out loud, and then laid down on the towel, stretched out languidly on her back like a Vargas painting in an old Playboy Magazine.

"Tell us more of the treasure story." Lana urged, from her seat in the fighting chair. I cleared my throat.

"Mel Fisher was an Indiana chicken farmer who eventually moved to California and opened the first dive shop in the state. In 1953, he married Dolores Horton who became his business partner. She was one of the first women to learn how to dive and set a women's record by staying underwater for 50 hours. Mel and Deo had five children: sons Terry, Dirk, Kim, and Kane, and daughter Taffi. In 1975, Mel's oldest son Dirk, his wife Angel, and one of the divers died after their boat sank due to bilge pump failure during their quest for treasure. Mel struggled through decades of hard times treasure hunting in the Florida Keys with the motto 'Today's the Day.'

Mel found the Spanish galleon Nuestra Señora de Atocha in 1985. The 'Atocha Motherlode' was worth over four hundred million dollars and included forty tons of gold and silver with over a hundred thousand Spanish silver coins known as 'pieces of eight'. They also found gold coins, Colombian emeralds, gold and silver artifacts, and silver ingots. Large as it was, this was roughly only half of the treasure that went down with the Atocha.

The wealthiest part of the ship, the stern castle, is yet to be found. Still missing according to copies of the ships manifest are over three hundred silver bars and some bronze cannons, among other things.

The United States government got greedy and tried to take most of the treasure. Mel sued and it went all the way to the United States Supreme Court. The Supreme Court of the United States confirmed Fisher's ownership of the recovered treasure and transferred ownership of seventy-five percent of the appraised value of everything recovered."

"It's amazing how much you know about the, what was the name of the ship?" Cindy exclaimed, having come up from the bow to hear the story. "You sound like a travelogue. You must have read a lot."

If she only knew. We trolled up and down the color change for hours and boated four decent dolphins, a thirty-pound Cobia, and released a sailfish that would have topped fifty pounds. On the way back the three of us, including Cindy who had made herself presentable in public again, munched our sandwiches. At the dock, the deck hand-cleaned our catch. That evening, after dining on fresh Cobia, we retired to the back yard for drinks and conversation. At about ten, the couple drained their last solo cup. They stood up, a little wobbly, hand in hand. Cindy whispered in Lana's ear. She gave a short nod, looking not that enthusiastic but apparently cooperative. Cindy turned to me with a sly smile.

And that's how I finally got my birthday present after all these years.

18
Eat, Drink and Remarry

Mostly, life was pretty routine. Quiet weeks, full weekends with most people using the inn as a base for major partying elsewhere. Many guests couldn't make the ten-thirty a.m. deadline for breakfast during weekends and managed only a banana or a bagel at the eleven a.m. checkout time. As an adults-only B&B, the poolside occasionally served as an impromptu site for extracurricular activities and I usually let people play (with me as an eager voyeur) unless another guest complained, which they rarely did. More likely when they saw the fun they offered to join in, which I equally enjoyed. But one weekend, the routine changed.

The whole inn was booked far in advance, selling out to a wedding party.

I didn't have a lot of responsibility at this cluster fuck. No special set up. Just a catering service that brought in lunch and a booze-on-wheels truck that brought in everything from Fresca to Fireball. For the officiant, they got a local girl. The last time I saw her she was about two and wouldn't know me from the man in the moon. I knew her folks well, and they would have blown my cover if they were around. Jim and Susan Ternal made a living having cats jump through flaming hoops in Mallory Square at sunset every night. They were the original millennial Hippies and named their daughter Hope. That wouldn't have been a biggie, except for her middle name they threw on her - Springsey. So we ended up with Hope Springsey Ternal. I'll bet she learned how to fight at Key West High with that moniker.

Saturday was the wedding day. The wedding planner showed up in the morning and she told me brusquely to stay out of her way, then started carrying out and setting up folding chairs on the back patio, five at a time, a feat even I suspected I was incapable of. I scurried. She was a large woman in comfortable shoes, if you get my drift, and it looked like she could fight dirty.

At about two the invited guests started to gather poolside, but the lovely couple was nowhere to be seen. Around three the blushing bride came down. She was fiftyish, over nourished, and wearing a classic white bridal dress four sizes too small, probably a relic from three weddings ago. She was wobbling on six-inch pumps and covered her face with a veil that I would have suggested she leave on after the ceremony. I would hazard a guess she had no business wearing white. Her makeup looked good at fifty feet. At ten feet, you could see she was made up to look good at fifty feet. She really should have worn something a little less low cut, at least enough to hide the "*Property of San Berdoo Hells Angels*" tattoo on her left breast, an honor I would have probably not been two proud of.

"Where's Chris and Clifford?" Was the first thing she said. From the slur in her voice, I could tell she was outside more than one vodka/cran already. "Chris! Clifford!" she called out for her twin seventeen-year-olds.

"Boss," Matilda whispered in my ear, "Last time I saw those boys, they were headed upstairs with the Maid of Honor." Glancing up toward the second floor, she added, "This is gonna get ugly."

About then the groom showed up at the pool. Choosing something a little less formal he was wearing a dirty aloha shirt, cutoffs with yesterday's Dolphin guts smeared on the front, flip flops, a Guy Harvey hat, and Carrera shades. "Ok let's get this over. It's halftime and the Chiefs are beating Dallas." About then a door opened upstairs and both boys emerged, hastily smoothing their hair and tucking in their shirts. Following behind them was the bridesmaid, also making hasty repairs. The blushing bride had something to blush about now. What a perfect Key West bridal ensemble.

You could sell tickets to this.

With everyone together, Hope figured it was now or never. She went through a pretty traditional set of "Do You's" and pronounced them husband and wife. That sent the groom stomping back up the stairs for the second half. At that point it might have moved into a normal reception had it not been for the two brothers and the bridesmaid beating a hasty retreat back up to their room, probably for sloppy seconds. At the top of the back stairs, I swear I saw a confederate grey uniform with Lieutenant Bars, just standing silent. The bride made a mad dash for the vodka and would have made it had she not caught one of her Fuck Me Please Pumps in a paver poolside and went headfirst into the pool. Undaunted, she slipped, the soggy gown overhead, tossed off her shoes, and emerged from the pool soaking wet in a white shelf bra, nylons, garter belt, and crotchless panties, which she chose to stay in for the rest of the reception. Last I saw of her, she was having a drink with the best man, and making quiet plans to sneak off with him for a quickie, once it got dark enough for nobody to see them.

I figured the ice cream cake was gonna last longer than the marriage.

Just saying.

19
Visit

It happened one night while I was drinking alone, poolside. First, a feeling I wasn't exactly alone, and then a *presence* manifested itself in an Adirondack chair a few feet away. Just like the painting – green satin dress gathered high at the waist, low cut bodice, hair piled high and secured with a tortoise shell comb, and a huge emerald and ruby cross around her neck, resting between ample beige cleavage. She sat there for a while, not even recognizing my existence for ten minutes before I decided to hazard speaking to her.

"Nice night out," I started.

"Why did you tear down my carriage barn?" She answered with a thick Spanish accent.

"Cause there ain't no more carriages and my guests like to swim. Haven't you noticed?"

She ignored the answer and went on. "And you have changed my house so much. I did not give permission for you to do that."

"It's not your house anymore. In fact, it's not even a house. It's an inn. And besides, you don't need it. Haven't you figured it out? You're dead."

"Who is dead?" She asked, "I am here, am I not?"

This was getting cray-cray. I wasn't sure how to answer.

"Haven't you realized you've hung around here for a very long time? And you can walk through walls? I understand you stay around because of the cross."

She changed the subject and ignored my questions entirely. "This cross has been part of the Galarza family for many generations. I must safeguard it."

"It was once part of a shipwreck," I remarked. "How did your family come by it?"

She sounded like a broken record.

"This cross has been part of the Galarza family for many generations. I must safeguard it."

That was going nowhere, so I changed the subject. "Does it concern you that you don't recognize anyone else here?"

"Oh, I do," she answered. I see Marcus frequently, and he gives me pleasure every week. Sadly, he lost his legs. I never asked him how."

I quickly realized her mistake. "Different Marcus. Probably his great-great-grandson. Do you mean to tell me he makes love to you regularly? Does he know you're a spirit?"

She didn't answer. I decided to change the subject. "You used to come to my bedroom often."

"That is my bedroom!" she retorted. "But I was asked not to, so no more."

Ah, that explains it. Lex got through to her, regardless of what she told me differently.

"But," she continued. "I sleep with other people. Often, but only one time each. I like to spread my charm around."

"You mean to say you've been shagging my guests? Just the men?" I asked. "How about the women?"

"I scare those *coño's*," she said, tossing her head. "Nobody enjoys men under my roof but Louisa Galarza."

No wonder my TripAdvisor scores have been so good.

And here I thought it was clean sheets and my bad jokes during cocktails.

Sheesh.

I thought it as good a time as any to pop the question.

"So where's the cross hidden?"

No answer, and just like that, I was all alone again.

The next day I caught Marcus in back trimming a huge philodendron tree. We exchanged pleasantries and talked about how fast plants grow in this tropical environment and all the various critters that come with them, including lizards, iguanas, and palmetto rats in the palm trees and roaches you could saddle and ride. At least the lizards keep the bugs at bay, and the king and gopher snakes help curb the rat population. After a few minutes of chit chat I decided to throw him a little curve.

"So," I started. "I hear you've been getting a little booty on the side." He paled and looked prepared to bolt. I put up both hands in a 'halt' gesture. "No reason to be scared, I don't mind you screwing a dead girl. Like they say, when it's good, it's great and when it's bad it's still great."

Marcus looked poised to run. "Honest boss, she just put it there in 'fron of me. I couldn't turn it down." The he hesitated and looked indignant. "Dead? They ain't nothing bout her that's dead." He looked indignantly at me. "Seriously, boss, I think I could tell the difference."

I sighed, and for what seemed like the umpteenth time, I led him into the house and introduced him to Louisa's picture. When I told him the story, and that she thought he was his own ancestor. Marcus turned about three shades lighter, which was quite a trick because he was about the darkest (and most handsome) Bahamian I had ever met. Then, he seemed to calm down and looked up towards the clouds. "Great grand pappy took a thirty-two caliber slug in the shoulder when he got caught tapping that if I recall the fambly tale." He grinned to himself. "I can tell you now it was probably worth it," he turned to me. "If she come back by, do you mind if I continue to take pleasure wit her? She's mighty fine pussy, even if'n she be a spirit."

"Hard, often, and heavy," I answered, nodding. "One thing for sure, you can't fuck her to death."

He walked away back to his philodendron, flashing me a big toothy smile.

20
Come as You Ain't

Like Karen and I found out before, Fantasy Fest was one time of the year I could walk about in public without any risk of being recognized. Courtesy of Amazon, I acquired a nice costume; Pirate shirt, tight pleather pants, suede boots, and a pirate's dreadlock wig. Add a fake earring, a stuffed parrot for my shoulder, a patch over one eye, and some black soot on my face, courtesy of the patio grille.

For extra effect, I planned to stuff a medium-size towel down one leg of my pants to keep the ladies following, and voila! Instant unrecognizable Bric. Despite the tight pants, it was pretty "PG" rated by Fantasy Fest standards, but the goal was to blend in, not stand out, and besides, sexy apparel that was appropriate for the bedroom, the swingers club and Duval Street during the last week of October was reserved for nubile young MILFs and hot boy toys, not senior citizens like me. Not to say there weren't lots of seniors that made the effort, and I applaud the attempt to dress younger than you should, but at a certain point in your life, it's touch but don't look instead of look but don't touch.

Three weeks before the holiday, I got a curve thrown at me, straight out of Oklahoma.

Karen

She's one of a half dozen people in the world that has my phone number. You could have knocked me down with a feather when I got a text in early October.

Karen: "Fancy some company for Fantasy Fest?"

Me: "Who's got a gun at your head?"

Karen: "Seriously. I feel like doing a little slumming. Is there room at the inn?"

Me: "Come on down. I'll make room."

She went on to give me an arrival date and asked what I would be wearing that week. I gave her the details, then realized my mouth wrote a check my butt couldn't cash; There *weren't* and rooms at the inn, and she didn't hint that *my* bed was a consideration. We were booked solid. I considered several alternatives, including becoming Scarlet's platonic bedpartner for a week, and then realized I did have a solution.

Karen arrived on the Wednesday before the Saturday parade, toting more luggage than she normally traveled with. I gave her a big hug and she returned the gesture with a 'kiss your brother' peck on the cheek. I led her up the micro elevator to my room. "Hey," she backed off. "This wasn't part of the invitation."

"I assure you, madam, my intentions are purely honorable." And led her by hand through the bedroom, and after tugging on the right items, we went through the bookcase into my private suite.

"Here you are, milady your own private castle. I'll be just out there a few steps away should you get lonely."

"I'll be sure to call if I find a monster in the closet," Karen answered, with a toss of her hair, "But I wouldn't hold my breath." I nodded in understanding, and we made plans to meet after dark in the lobby, in full costume.

As agreed, we met later to crawl Duval, and no two finer pirates ever paired up. I was dressed in my finery, and Karen went all out. She sported knee-length boots, and a denim skirt slit to the hip with a leather thong lacing up both sides. Fishnet poked under the skirt, held up by a black garter belt. A puffy-sleeved pirate shirt matched mine but was cut so low in front, the dark edge of both areolas peeked out of the blouse. She caught my gaze and explained. "I'm normally a little more conservative than this, but I can promise you nobody that might recognize me will be looking at my eyes."

She topped off the outfit with a tri-corner hat, one blacked-out tooth, and a fake scar on her cheek that looked real enough to suggest she go for stiches.

We strolled down Duval Street and it was a surreal experience. We recognized or would have been recognized by just about every local we saw standing behind a food booth or in front of one, drinking. It took some serious effort not to stop and shake hands or hug dozens of people, many who I either grew up with or had intimate encounters with over the years. We stopped in at Buzzards for a drink and we sat way in the back in a dark corner. I looked longingly at the corner closet where my long-gone Gibson Ripper Bass used to be stored. Bored of the activity or lack thereof, we walked along the dock and took a seat at Schooner Wharf. A comely server that I briefly dated asked for my order, thankfully not recognizing us. She was dressed in about ten square inches of pirate costume, leaving little to the imagination. "Vodka-OJ for two," I ordered, to disconnect my usual choice of Titos and cran, less she put two and two together. When she served our drinks, she leaned way over to reveal her cleavage down clear to her navel, probably her way of coaxing out a larger tip. For a moment, she looked at me in a puzzled way, as if she recognized me. Maybe my eyes, or eye, as I had a pirate's patch over one. I quickly looked away, and she shrugged and walked off. After a few drinks and listening through a set with Mike Mcloud, I dropped a ten in the tip bucket and we stepped away from the bar with our tri-corner pirate hats pulled over our eyes.

We crawled back up Duval Street, stopping to pay homage at Sloppy Joes and listen to a few songs with Barry Cuda, and then painfully abused our tired knees by walking up the stairs to the Garden of Eden at the top of the Bull and Whistle. I paid my cover charge, which they only assess during Fantasy Fest, and bought a couple of overpriced Titos and cran. Nobody there knew us.

On normal weekend nights, the Garden is populated with mostly locals and a few tourists, usually trying to coax their wife/girlfriend out of their garments, and then get fiercely angry if anyone looks at them, much less move in. What would you expect? I ordered our second drinks and scanned the herd. Naked guys looking for other guys, topless female tourists sitting shyly, and in the middle of the patio, a couple, about my age, him sitting on a bench and her, fully dressed in a Hawaiian style top and a full skirt, sat next to him. It was fairly normal until she slid her hand up the skirt, exposed herself, boldly, and stared right at me. I stared right back, tipped my drink toward them in a mock toast, and saluted.

That's how you could tell locals from tourists. The tourists were here off the chain. Anything goes, and probably did. Locals were a bit more discrete – not to say they didn't get twisted but they just didn't make a spectacle of themselves doing it. A quiet word, an offered drink, a subtle hint, and off you would go.

This went on for the rest of the week, meeting Karen in the

parlor about dark, all costumed up, for a night on the town. I changed it up every night, sometimes as a pirate, and sometimes as a mobster in a full-length leather coat, courtesy of a hotel guest who had to leave in haste in the middle of the night to avoid castration by an enraged boyfriend. Karen reprised her nun outfit from a few years ago, with the front in demure habit, and the back completely sheer from head to toe, with only a tiny triangle of black lace panty underneath. There was no shortage of parties or crowds to get lost in. I was having a good time, and I think so was she, but it was more like a weekend with a distant cousin than someone I once proposed to.

We skipped the Saturday parade completely and ended our Fantasy Fest experience on Friday. The last event we dropped in on; we really fit into. Since Pat Croce's Rum Barrel was gone, the pirate bash had moved to the Turtle Kraals, and we spent a few hours perched on barstools, with me looking out of the corner of my un-patched eye, ogling at the scantly-dressed pirate wenches and a couple dozen Jack Sparrows busy trying to get in their pants, or under their skirts. After a few hours, the crowd became wall to wall, so we left and took Simonton back to Fleming Street at about midnight. I invited Karen to join me for a poolside nightcap and to my surprise, she nodded agreement. Neither of us was feeling any pain at that point. At a quiet moment, I leaned across the Adirondack chair and gently kissed her.

She returned the kiss. Somewhat reluctantly, and leaned away, sipping her drink.

"No, Bric. There's too much water under that bridge. That chapter's behind us."

Ooh, I thought, *thanks for picking the scab off my heart.* Breaking the awkward silence, she asked, with a sweeping gesture of one arm, "How do you like this?"

"Oh, it's a living," I answered, somewhat deflated. "You meet nice people, have great conversations, and live a little calmer life. I like it."

I couldn't tell what she said next was Karen or the vodka. "I have to believe you must hate it," she answered. "Russel Bricklin Wahl, the center of the universe, having to change your name, hiding from everybody you know. You have to be the baby at the baptism, the bride at the wedding and the coffin at the funeral." She swept her arm around again. "It's got to be miserable being a nobody cook in a nobody bed and breakfast. I'm sure you will figure out a way to break what ain't broken, either that or trouble will come looking for you."

I didn't have an answer for her. Maybe she hit the nail on the head.

We drank in silence. A little later, without another word, she got up from her chair and went up the back stairs to her room.

The next morning, while I was downstairs cooking breakfast, she must have left. She didn't stay for the rest of Fantasy Fest, and she didn't even say goodbye.

During those five days in October, I always had the inn booked full with a decent rate. I chose not to charge those dog-robber prices some places charged like the La Concha charged Karen and me a few years ago. I priced the rates at just about twice normal (I'm dumb but not stupid), and I was happy. We sold out a year in advance and always got a lot of regulars. I kind of picked and chose my clientele. Happy people, straight or gay, here for a good time and not a stupid time. People that came to have fun and not get too crazy and a smattering of good-looking single MILFs that, along with a willingness to wear nothing but body paint most of the time, liked to crawl in the sack with yours truly at least once.

Ah, the bennies of the job.

Sometimes my regulars had to cancel at the last minute, and I would suddenly come up with an opening. I ended up with a vacancy just a few days before the start of festivities, and Scarlet, who had been responding with 'no vacancy' for months, booked what turned out to be a gay couple, Gary and Royce, two funeral directors from Ft Lauderdale. They got in the spirit right away and disrobed in the cab on the way from the airport. Walking up to the front desk with nothing on but sandals, they immediately hit on Scarlet and invited him to join them. They were firmly, but politely, set straight, so to speak. "We'd like a room with two queens," Ray announced. "Sorry boys, all we have is rooms with king beds," replied Scarlet. "Ok then," Ray answered. "We'd like a king bed," he giggled. "With two queens!" Scarlet shrugged and checked them in. "Just an FYI, you can't be walkin around outside waving yo Willie, even in the 'zone'. We don't care what you do around here, except you shouldn't doin' the high hard one outdoors in sight of others, but." She continued, "Yo need to wear somepin dat covers yo dick when in public. Otherwise yo be sleepin' someplace else tonight, and get free breakfast, complements of Monroe County Sheriffs."

"Why?" Asked Ray, "I see lots of bare titties everywhere. Why should it matter?"

"Because the people that make the laws are all men and they like titties," answered Scarlet. "Jes play by da rules 'an you'll be fine. I see you booked a romance package," Scarlet continued. "That includes champagne and chocolate strawberries, which will be delivered shortly, and breakfast in bed tomorrow morning, providing you're still here and not in da pokey."

"Do you have triple rates?" Asked Greg, hopefully. "We hope to get lucky tonight and bring a bed partner home with us."

Scarlet turned toward me and I offered a supplement number after thinking for a minute, and then headed for the kitchen to start preparing the strawberries. As I have said before, Key West's facts beat anyplace else's fiction.

Triple rates for a romance package.

Sheesh.

21
Bike Week

The people that really run Key West, (*not the politicians, they just dig up sewer lines during tourist season),* but the real people that run the town, namely a handful of businessmen, carefully peruse their calendars for opportunities. That means the quiet times of the year when they can invent holidays. That's the real reason Fantasy Fest is in October when the weather, humidity, and chance for rain with a name is much less attractive than peak season in February or March. I know, Fantasy Fest is kind of an offshoot of Mel Fisher's parties that he used to hold, but the reason it got so big was that it was held at a super dead time.

That goes for September too. It's still hot, steamy, and at the peak of hurricane season. The kids are back in school and the town is deado. That's why, forty-four years ago a Miami Motorcycle dealer dreamed up the Poker Run to spiff up business during the off-season. He created an event that started on the mainland Saturday morning and ran down the keys all day. The bikers would stop at bars and restaurants on the way and draw cards. When they got to Key West, they would dress up for a big dinner and play their poker hands for prizes. There would be other contests on Sunday morning before they headed back, including best-dressed couple and riding contests, like riding over a teeter-totter.

Today, the event has morphed into a massive extravaganza, with over fifteen thousand riders and I had the inn booked full with a very eclectic group of businessmen. They would trailer their show-stopper chrome Harley and Indian choppers to the edge of town, unload them, and ride the into town, pulling into the bed and breakfast en masse, their faces screwed up in agony from sitting on tiny seats not meant to be actually used for a whole two miles.

Baggage, trophy wives, and significant others arrived in civilized fashion, via SUV, with nary a hair out of place nor a nail broken. The riders valued their chrome-plated, custom-painted masterpieces at least a notch above their women and wanted to park their bikes out back by the pool every night, much to Bela's distaste. He would be cleaning up crankcase oil for weeks. I think they would take the bikes to bed if they would fit in the elevator. All weekend, these would be bikers would motor from bar to bar, wives, and girlfriends dutifully tagging along in their SUVs, all dressed like Playboy centerfolds.

Since they had the whole inn bought out, I didn't have much issue when the leader approached me and asked to hold a "special" event Saturday night. "It's kind of an initiation ceremony. Everyone that joins has to do it." I told him as long as everyone was in agreement, and it was safe I was okay. What followed late that evening was bizarre. Suddenly gone were a bunch of straight-arrow businessmen, and in their place they had transformed into outlaw bikers, complete with black boots, laced halfway up the calf greasy jeans and vests, flying a club name and 'colors'. Around eleven, an outsider rode into the backyard on a rather plain Jane Harley. He dismounted as did his girlfriend. The fact his bike could seat two already set him aside from the members. He took the girl by the hand and led her poolside, where she stood, hand at her side. You could tell, as excited and aroused as everyone else looked, she sincerely looked like she wished she was someone else. "C'mon girl, let's see what you've got!" yelled the leader. Slowly and shyly, she first took off her blouse and then kicked off her sandals before unbuttoning her pants. Standing in bra and panties, she folded her arms across her chest, and then put her hands up to her eyes. "I can't!" she cried.

"You promised," said her boyfriend. "They won't let me join unless you do!" She stood by the pool, arms tightly clasped around her waist, and nodded, teary-eyed. Slowly reaching behind her back, she unclasped her bra, letting it fall to the floor. Quickly stepping out of her bikini panties, she stood in the light of the tiki torches, covering herself as best she could, shivering in shame. "Who wants the first blowjob?" asked the leader. "Hey, that wasn't part of the deal!" Exclaimed the boyfriend. "You said I had to bring a girl and have her strip. Nobody said anything about any sex."

"The initiation rules have changed tonight," slurred the leader. "Everybody gets a blowjob, or you don't get in the club."

Watching from upstairs on the second-floor balcony, I was about to step in. This wasn't nice or healthy. I took two steps down the stairs when I felt a cold wind and an icy hand on my shoulder.

"Wait," came a voice. At that moment, the girl took her hands away from her face, and proudly tipped her head back. "This is important to me too," she said. "Who's first?"

The club leader stood up and unzipped. With his belly, I doubt he'd seen his equipment firsthand in a dozen years. "Come to Papa," he ordered. Obediently, she approached him. Kneeling on a towel, she took him in her mouth. It was every bit of ten seconds before he let out a groan and his knees buckled. She wiped her mouth and turned to the rest of the crowd. "Who's next?" It sounded defiant, almost a croak. There were fully ten men around the pool, but only four stood up, the others either too drunk to perform or too married to dare. She took each one to climax and then stood up, drinking heavily from an offered beverage. She turned to reach for her strewn garments and the club leader ordered, "Wait, who said you're through? Some of us might want a little more."

I'd seen all I wanted. I went to my room and got my Glock out of the bedroom nightstand. Waking out to the top of the steps, I fired a shot from the balcony. I quietly apologized to the ancient Banyan tree for using it for target practice, but I didn't want to fire in the air and cause damage, or even worse, bodily harm to something, or someone.

"That's enough," I shouted from the balcony. "Initiation or not, there'll be no more of that on this property. Miss, please get dressed." I casually used the Glock as a pointer and motioned to the boyfriend. "No club that has this kind of rules should have you as a member. Take her out of here and give some thought as to whom you want to hang around with."

The girl took my cue, hastily pulled on her pants, and slid into her top. Shoving her bra and panties into her jeans pockets, the boyfriend punched the electric starter and they rode off in a roar. I turned to the club members, some of whom still had their zippers down. "I'd kick the rest of you out right now, but you're too drunk to ride and the whole town is full. Party's over. No breakfast in the morning. If anyone wants a refund come see me at the desk before you leave. I don't want your money."

22
Nothing is Forever

I have no idea how it started. I will swear Louisa knocked over an antique oil lamp in the reading room on purpose. The sprinklers came on, but they were no match for the guts of a wooden building that had been drying in the tropics for a hundred and fifty years. The Key West Fire Department, who I have always claimed have never lost a foundation in over a century, came as quick as possible, but by the time they got here, Nobody's Inn was fully involved from top to bottom.

I managed to grab my box of goodies that held my gold Escudos, a few pieces of eight, and the 1715 bezel-wrapped doubloon that was once around Matt Black's neck. The fire department concentrated on keeping surrounding structures from catching fire and watched the old mansion burn to the ground. It's ironic that Wendy's family home succumbed to the same fate as my ancestral home saw decades earlier. Fortunately, there was only one guest at the time, a rotund, fiftyish lady with a yappy toy poodle. She ran out wearing nothing but a tee shirt and flip flops, screaming bloody murder, though the fire was slow enough she would have had time to dress for the Oscars, makeup included. The staff fought the fire for ten minutes, and when they figured out it was a losing battle, gathered up what they could and backed up to the street to watch Key West's finest botch the rest of the effort.

The firemen wasted time and endangered my staff while they searched for the source of the raucous laughter that was coming from upstairs. I would guess Louisa literally, got the last laugh. They never found a body up there. It took three days before all the hot spots cooled off, and I sent in a crew to clean up. I had no doubt they wouldn't find anything worth salvaging.

My half-million dollar kitchen had sagged into a Salvador Dali scene, and the painting of Louisa Galarza that I had rescued once was reduced to ash. The only thing I saved was the Ulu knife I bought in Alaska years ago. The hard metal and fossilized Mammoth tusk handle was found sitting peacefully on the window sill in its stone holder, miraculously intact as if it possessed a spell.

It wasn't till then that we remembered the garage. When we got out in back, we found the garage, and my Firebird pride and joy had been fully involved. I cried over that car. You could always build another house, but my Smokey and the Bandit Special could probably never be replaced.

I sold the burned-out hulk and lot to some unsuspecting entrepreneur, ghost, and all, who planned on building condos. I made more money on the lot than I spent buying and refurbishing Nobody's Inn. I think I could have settled the National Debt. But I was effectively homeless.

Rumpy offered me a room in his new place up on Big Pine at a monthly price that nearly gave me a heart attack. He said he would waive the deposit as well as first and last and only charge an arm for rent instead of an arm and a leg, being we were business partners and stuff. What a big heart. He did warn me that the first time I went Brokeback Mountain on him my ass would be in the street. I calmly advised him, "I'm not of that persuasion, but if I do jump the fence, you will be the first person I call."

I wasn't quite ready to sit in a rocking chair with a quilt over my legs until I fell off Rumpy's porch one day and broke my freakin neck. Time to peruse the Help Wanted Ads in the Key West Citizen and the personals. Here's one *"Hermaphrodites of the world, throw off your chains. You have nothing to lose"* Well, if I were a hermaphrodite, I would certainly join that club. I hear that all hyenas sport both sexual organs.

No wonder hyenas are always laughing.

I kept looking, Help Wanted, Short Order Cook – nope. Don't wanna be someone's slave tossing greasy burgers for eight hours a day. Ah, Mel Fishers Company was looking for another treasure diver. Been there. Done that. Got the tee shirt.

Here we go. Chef on a hundred and thirty foot yacht. Owners are richer than Mickey Mouse and sail about once a month. The rest of the time you hang around, boat watch, and eat on their nickel. Must be able to cook a diverse selection. References? Lessee. Rumpy and Scarlett. I gotta find Scarlet's new number.

I can cook anything so long as it's Cajun.

Well, maybe a few other things.

Before I embarked on any other adventure, I had one last piece of unfinished business. I borrowed a bicycle and spent two days cruising Old Town before I found what I was looking for. I dialed Rumpy's number on my cell. "Rump, there's a shotgun house a block off White Street. They are asking six twenty five. It looks ratty enough; I bet you can squeeze them a bit." Rumpy was curious. "What do you want with another fixer-upper?" he asked. "Didn't you suffer enough last time?"

"It's not for me," I answered. I'll explain later. "Offer five-fifty cash, with a two-week escrow. I bet they bite." I gave him the address and hung up.

Two weeks later we owned a historic Key West shotgun home for five seventy five. My next bike ride took a little more effort, pedaling my ass all the way to Stock Island. I asked around the hood and it only took five minutes before the description of the people I was looking for struck pay dirt. I knocked on the door of a rundown single-wide. I heard the low "ruff" as Cousin Eddie twigged that an old friend was at the door. A diminutive voice called from inside; "We don't want any!" I yelled through the door. "Matilda, it's Russell Philips!" The answer came from inside, "Oh, just a moment Mr. Phillips!" and I heard the sounds of hasty tidying. The door opened and Bela ushered me in. Eddie raised his head a fraction of an inch, recognized me, and went back to sleep. So much for enthusiastic greetings. The inside of the house looked nothing like the outside. I expected a trailerhood interior but was greeted with an immaculately clean, well-maintained living room. "Nice." I admired as I sat down on the threadbare, but clean sofa. A calico cat immediately jumped in my lap and offered her ass up for a sniff. Apparently, Eddie has been convinced that this was an acceptable resident. "Stinky! Get down!" Matilda commanded. "Oh, that's okay," I countered. "I like cats and it's been a while since I got to pet one." After niceties were exchanged, Bela explained. "We keep the outside looking like that so we don't get broken into. Crooks ignore us because they think the inside is the same way." Bela, despite his Down Syndrome, was high-functioning. His speech was just a little clipped. "Mr. Phillips, why you visit?" he asked abruptly. He wasn't unhappy I had dropped by, but he instinctively knew that it wasn't just a social call.

"A long time ago, both of you told me you were saving up for a house. Remember Mister Rumpy who used to drop by Nobody's Inn? I think he has a house he might want to sell. How much do you have saved up?"

"We have over three hundred thousand dollars in the bank," answered Matilda. "It's a lot of money, but not nearly enough to buy a house in Key West. We might never have enough, but we still save every penny. That much has taken fifteen years." She held up her head proudly. "We don't want a condo." She looked at her husband proudly. "Bela likes to fix things." He had walked out of the room, and Matilda leaned over and whispered in my ear. "There might not be enough time," she said. "People with Down Syndrome sometimes don't live much past fifty."

I nodded with an understanding smile and went on. "This house is a little run-down but livable. You might be able to give it a little TLC. Are you both working?"

"Yes, with your recommendation we got on at another little B & B in old town. We start Monday." I smiled with relief and fished a piece of paper out of my pocket. "Here's the address. My friend told me that the back door was unlocked. Go take a look and let me know what you think."

Bela took the address from me and studied it like it was the secret recipe for Coca-Cola. "We'll catch the downtown bus tomorrow and go look, but even if it needs fixing, nobody will give us a loan."

"Just go take a look and let me worry about the little stuff," I answered.

After leaving, I gave Rumpy a call. "Bela and Matilda are going to look at the shotgun house," I started. I'm going to let them have it for four twenty-five." I went on to explain my plan.

"Four twenty-five?" he exclaimed. "We paid five seventy-five. I walked through it. The place needs some minor plumbing, a little re-wiring, and paint. I couldn't find any termites, and all the appliances appear to work. With a little effort, we can easily get seven, six fifty at the least." He paused for a moment. "What are you doing buy high, sell low? Using new math?"

"I walked through it too and I agree with what you found. The place is small but sound. It's time for me to pay it forward. Let's just say I'm trying to earn a little corner in heaven," I answered. "Use my funds please, and let me know when it's all set." I finished with a few more instructions.

Rumpy grumbled an 'okay' and hung up. Two days later, I dropped by the trailer hood and paid another visit.

Matilda was as animated as I've ever seen her. "It's just perfect, Mr. Phillips! Bela looked it over and said it only needs a little cleanup." Then she put her head down and looked sad. "But there's no way to buy it."

"I heard through the grapevine that Mr. Rumpy is motivated to sell," I explained. "Offer him four hundred and twenty-five thousand, and ask him to carry the mortgage." I thought about the monthly payment. "What are you paying for this dump, ah fine establishment?"

"We pay nine hundred a month, plus utilities. That's why the air conditioner is always turned off." Bela spoke up. "Air conditioning costs too much money."

"I'll put a word into Mr. Rumpy to charge you eight hundred a month," I answered. "Oh, and ask him to pay for closing costs."

They both sat dumbfounded. Christmas, the tooth fairy, and the fairy godmother all just shined over them. I got up to leave, and Matilda jumped up and gave my legs a big hug. "You keep saying Mister Rumpy is doing this, but I know where this is really coming from," she said. "You are a good man, Mr. Phillips."

"Nonsense," I answered. "I can't afford that house, myself. Now I'll arrange for Mr. Rumpy to be at the house tomorrow at five-thirty. That should give you plenty of time to get there by the Key West Transit. The stop is only a block away on White Street." I got down on my knees and hugged Matilda back, then solemnly shook Bela's hand. "I'll drop by occasionally to check on Mr. Rumpy's investment." I shook my finger at them. "Don't disappoint him." I cautioned them. "Don't you worry," Bela answered. "We will never miss a payment. We promise."

ALEGRE

23
Ship's Chef

Well, I guess either my friends told good lies or I passed the cooking test. Macadamia crusted yellowtail snapper, shrimp and scallop stuffed Portobello mushroom caps and a pear, crumbled gorgonzola, candied black walnut field green salad with raspberry vinaigrette dressing. Either that or nobody else wanted to be on a twenty-four-hour call and be around to stock a yacht with three days, three weeks, or three months' worth of groceries. Yes, months. Despite the understanding that this was a once-a-month job, the Smythes seemed to suddenly find more free time and would jet off to Venice on a moment's notice and have the boat run over to pick them up to cruise back. Or vice-versa. The yacht, or rather ship was very sea-worthy and capable of handling all but the roughest seas. We were smart enough to avoid the Atlantic during all of the hurricane season, and most of the time the ocean was as smooth as a rubber ducky bathtub.

Yes Smythe. Julian and Edwina, but I called them Thurston and Lovey in my head. Mr. Smythe was bald, fat-ish, and tended to occasionally sneak below decks with young deckhands named Alberto. Mrs. Smythe was well north of fifty, chubby, and very fond of her vodka. Mr. Smythe was a teetotaller and Mrs. Smythe hated to drink alone so I obliged whenever asked, right up to but not including the point where all I could prepare for a hot meal was chipped beef on toast.

I had fallen asleep and woke up in the middle of a Harlequin novel.

Well, I hope the author writes me in for several sequels.

One day she brought up a big bag of clothes and asked me to take them to Goodwill. "Why don't you just throw them out?" asked her husband. "People in Africa are starving," she answered. "I assure you, anyone that can wear those clothes isn't starving," answered her husband. She walked off in a huff to the sanctity of her vodka. I headed out to find a Goodwill drop and Julian scurried downstairs to his cabin boy harem.

Unlike hubby, Lovey didn't shit in her own nest, sticking to vodka for her sins. She never got dressed and usually wore all day what she slept in the night before, a thin nightgown and bedroom mules, with large pendulous breasts swaying in the daylight underneath thin sheer silk. I suspected at first, that my cooking duties included servicing her but she never came on to me and treated her scanty attire like it was perfectly normal daytime wear. Since most of the crew were hand-picked by Mr. Smythe and tended, by choice to play for the other team, I guess it was no biggie. If she knew of her husband's transgressions, she didn't seem to take issue of it or mind. They were cordial to each other but spent zero time together. She was half in the bag every day by noon, and I doubted her liver would outlast the marriage.

Any time they were in Key West, Mr. Smythe would encourage his wife to fly up to Miami, where she could practice her hobby as a professional consumer, spending thousands in Aventura or Bal Harbor, although I guessed it must have been all on nightwear, as that's about all I ever saw her wear. While she was out of town, the old man went farming on the south end of Duval Street, frequenting such places as La Te Da or Bourbon Street Pub, where he quickly gained a reputation as a generous man among the countless beautiful young men who hung around.

Keyword "hung."

We stuck around the Caribbean off and on for most of the summer. I worked on my tan during the day and enjoyed flavored Deep Eddy Vodka with the Missus in the evening. All I had to do was keep both of them fat and happy, not a problem for both of them, supplementing the freezer with fresh seafood bought from local fishermen who dropped by frequently hoping both to sell some fresh catch and catch a glimpse of 'Lovey's' lack of apparel, even though the view wasn't that appetizing. With a little fresh Mahi or Wahoo on the menu, I could conjure up meals that would do justice on Madison Avenue, even better because it went from ocean to table on the same day.

Once I turned a fresh caught yellow fin tuna into a chilled black and white sesame crusted appetizer, complete with teriyaki /wasabi dip on a bed of lettuce and pickled ginger. They loved that so much they wanted to share and called for Mr. Smythe's sister's niece to come down for the summer. I didn't relish the thought of having to babysit some finicky brat all summer, but figured that was the price of paradise. Two days later we motored the yacht up to Port Everglades to pick up "Missy." I spent the day shopping for fresh veggies you couldn't find in Key West, and when I got back, our guest was on board. So I was wrong. The Smythes had talked about their sister's niece like she was five or six, and she might have been twenty years ago. Draped across a chaise lounge on the top deck was a vision of South Beach beauty, wearing fifty-four cents of leather bikini. She tipped her glasses off her nose, labeled me as "the help" as I had an armload of veggie-filled grocery bags, and went back to her sun.

It went like that for the rest of the summer. I never got her real name; The Smythes only called her Missy; I named her the Ice Princess. She spent days on the sun deck in that teeny bikini, sometimes just the bottoms, and seemed to enjoy my obvious agony as I served both her and Lovey drinks several times daily, painfully avoiding staring at her round, no tan line, pert little milkers. Lovey seemed to ignore the show, drinking herself blind on a chaise, under an umbrella. Since she had a niece for company, I didn't get invited to the evening drink fests, and I had to manage my vodka drinking solo every night.

As the song goes, some people think I may have a drinking problem. I think it's a solution.

This chicken dance went on for a few months, with me being relegated back to being just a cook, when one afternoon I passed Missy on the top deck, sunbathing face down. It appeared she hadn't even bothered to bring her top above deck.

"Care for a drink?" I dutifully offered. I wasn't really a waiter, but I was cordial and bored. Normally I just brought drinks when the old lady was around but she was nowhere in sight, probably stumble-drunk in her cabin.

"Vodka with a nano-splash of cran," she said almost

dismissively. I went to the bar and mixed her a drink and one for myself, and brought them out. "Put some oil on my back," she ordered. *Uh oh, the sex scene in Debbie Does Yhe Cabin Boy starts in a few more minutes.* I sat down on the edge of the lounge and cupped a little coconut oil in my left hand. Dutifully, I rubbed oil between her shoulders, while she rose up and sipped her drink from a straw. I had resisted putting a little paper umbrella in the drink. She sipped and nodded approval. "Excellent" she complimented, the first positive words I'd heard her utter since boarding. 'More," she commanded. "Put some on my legs and thighs." Act Two, Scene One. *The cook rubs her legs with coconut oil, and then slowly slides his hand to her crotch.* I knew better. She would probably cry "rape" so fast my head would spin and I would end up on a dock in Miami with my thumb out in two hours.

"How did you end up with this job?" she asked. "You aren't a fag, so my uncle has no use for you."

"I made the mistake of answering a want ad," I answered. "I had good references, and they like what I cook. Maybe nobody else applied."

"Where would you be if you weren't here?" she continued. "Flipping burgers or tending bar in some Key West dive, living in a moth-eaten single-wide trailerhood?"

I decided not to tell her I could almost buy a yacht this big with the cash I had in the bank.

"Something like that," was all I answered.

She rolled over and sat up, making no movement to cover her body. She sounded almost bored like she wanted me to fetch her a pair of slippers. She slid her bottoms down part way. "Fuck me. Here. Now."

I tried my best to look casual. "Here? Shouldn't we go below decks and find someplace a little more discrete?"

"It's more fun up here," she answered. "Aunt Edwina's sleeping with Prince Valium and won't wake up for hours. Uncle's below with some cabin boy's dick up his ass. C'mon, before I change my mind. You're starting to bore me. Or are you a fag too?"

"Nope," I responded. "Red-blooded American straight guy. I'm just not accustomed to jumping the boss's niece." I pointed up toward the helm. "The skipper might squeal."

"Oh I did him yesterday," she quipped. "He prefers boys but he got enthusiastic when I told him if he didn't play, I would cry to uncle that he tried to rape me." She looked square in my eyes. "And the same goes for you. If you don't play along, back you go to that single-wide." I slid off my shorts and joined her on the lounge. "Well, we wouldn't want that to happen, would we?"

Act Two Scene Two. The cabin boy roughly embraced her, ripping her bikini bottoms aside with one motion. Thrusting his blood-gorged love muscle deep into her freshly shaved love valley, he pounded her loins for ten minutes amid screams of joy, and exploded in a fit of ecstasy....

The ship's chef job lasted a whole two more months. One morning, long after Missy had headed back to her permanent occupation of college leech, they found Edwina in bed, the victim of her own excess. I learned she died from fatty myocardial degeneration due to obesity, the same affliction as what befell Momma Cass Elliot. We were cruising off the coast of Cypress and the old man, in mock grief, had her cremated and then had her ashes flown to her relatives in Detroit. About three days after the dearly departed, ah, departed, Mr. Smythe sent word by way of the captain that my services were no longer needed. He would pay for a one-way ticket back home to Key West, or if I wanted, I could be put ashore at the nearest port. I guess with the missus out of the way he wanted to populate the ship with his own personal harem. Based on his apparent lifestyle, I didn't fit in. I asked for an immediate release and cash equaling the cost of a plane ticket from Cypress to Miami

Two hours later I was standing on the dock with my backpack, one change of clothes in a plastic trash bag over my shoulder, and five hundred eighty-two dollars in my pocket. I didn't really need the cash, but it would be fun to play with house money for a few days.

I took a ferry to the fabled island of Lesbos that afternoon and spent a few weeks trying to convert lesbians, but all I could find were willing women with hairy armpits in need of a shower. Any women closer to my generation had hairy armpits, a mustache and smelled like old potatoes, even after they had been swimming in salt water. They all looked like versions of Harry Sykas with tits. Combine that scenario with the tendency for clothing-optional bathing on rock strewn beaches and I was going to need more than five hundred eighty two dollars' worth of therapy when I got home.

I don't think they made that much Ouzo.

After a few weeks working on language skills and endeavoring not to contract any life-ending STD's, I caught a boat to Naples and booked a flight to Key West, via Rome, Munich, Atlanta, and Miami. There are quicker ways to get home than that, but I'm superstitious and wanted to fly a domestic carrier.

The last time I went through customs in Atlanta, I ran afoul of the feds. This time I wasn't wanted, but they were intensely curious as to why this Yankee was flying one way via half the airports in the free world, with no checked bags. I got pulled into a room and was subjected to a rather inglorious body cavity search by a Sally Field lookalike in the presence of a poorly shaved gorilla whose sole duty was to make sure I played nice. I would assume they chose a more petite customs agent to perform the search so she could get her arm up my ass to the elbow. Actually, I'm sure it was just a finger or two, but after she didn't find any contraband I did ask if we were going steady now.

Along with the search of my person and belongings, drug-sniffing dogs were brought in and they swabbed every article of clothing, my dive watch, shave kit, wallet, sunglass case and spare hat. The money in my wallet tested positive, but they said that was pretty normal. Over eighty percent of the hundred-dollar bills in circulation outside the US tested positive for cocaine.

After two hours of the fifth degree, they grudgingly declared me clean. I think they were truly disappointed they found nothing. I ruined their day. Of course, they felt much better that I missed the connection to Miami. It wasn't their problem. It's the price I paid for being a suspect, innocent or not.

I spent the night on the floor at the airport. I could have splurged for a suite across the runway at the Hilton, but after the rooms on Lesbos, the carpet at the airport in Atlanta felt like a feather bed.

24
Be Careful What You Ask For

On the benefit of having all my downline connections canceled due to being a no-show, even though it wasn't my fault, I didn't land back in Key West till the following afternoon. I blasted out into the front of the airport terminal like Kramer in a Seinfeld show, into air so thick you could cut it. Ah, great to be back home again. Suddenly I realized all I had were sixty Euros in my pocket and not even a US dime, no car, no home, and not even a phone. I then noticed that I wasn't alone. Standing curbside was a vision of beauty, peering intently into her Droid. She had to be a model. Nobody else would get off a plane in Key West in a black micro skirt, long-sleeved white silk blouse, and five-inch fuck me heels. She couldn't have been much more than twenty. Tall, at least five-nine, and a slender, almost boyish figure.

I decided to take a shot. "Excuse me miss, but I lost my phone. (Several months ago). Could I borrow yours to make a local call?" I was waiting for the "Get lost, pervert!" response when she stopped texting and handed me her phone. "Sure. I'm supposed to be picked up but my flight got mixed up and I got here two hours early. I don't even know how to reach the guy that's supposed to pick me up. I'm here for the Miss Key West Beauty Pageant."

Beauty contest. It figures. Amazing body and probably the brain of a turnip. I thanked her and stepped into the shadows of the building so I could see the dial pad. I wracked my mind for Rumpy's number and took a shot out of the cobwebs in my brain. The phone was covered in pink flowers and smelled like the bottom of my grandma's purse. After three rings, I heard good news and bad. Fortunately, I had the right number. Unfortunately, it hit his voicemail. Fortunately, the airport has a bar. "Greetings. Rumpy here. Sorry I missed your call. If it's Monday, I'm at the doctor's getting the plumbing Roto rootered. If it's Tuesday, I'm on Marvin Key doing something I shouldn't be doing with someone I shouldn't be doing it with. If it's Wednesday, I'm hosting the Lower Keys

Ladie's Dolphin Derby with more girls than you can shake a stick at and won't be home till dark, or later if I get lucky. If it's Friday, Saturday, or Sunday I'll be hosting the Miss Key West Beauty Contest and have much better things to do than talk to you. If it's Thursday and I didn't answer, then I don't recognize this number and you're shit out of luck. Leave a message."

Sheesh. That wasn't a voicemail answer. That was the Gettysburg Address.

"Miss," I asked, with my hand over the phone. "What day is this?" I hadn't needed to know what day it was for months.

"Why, it's Thursday," she answered, looking puzzled.

I put the phone back to my ear. "Rump, it's..." I turned away from the girl and cupped the phone with my hand. "It's Bric. I'm at Key West Airport. Come get me. I'll be in the Conch Flyer. And I hit the end button. I handed the phone back and thanked the model. I started to head back into the air conditioning when suddenly it came to me. "Miss the person that's supposed to pick you up isn't named Mister Rumpendorfer, by chance?"

She looked astonished. "How did you know? He's running the Miss Key West Pageant. I don't check into the hotel till tomorrow, but this was the only cheap flight available. My Rumpendorfer was gracious enough to pick me up and offer me his spare room for the night. He's not a judge or anything so I was sure it's okay." I nodded knowingly. That's like putting the wolf in charge of the sheep. I explained to her, "I just got ahold of Mister Rumpendorfer's voicemail. I assure you he will be at the airport shortly and will be most happy to put you up. I held out my arm. In the meantime would you like to join me for an air-conditioned beverage? You are of legal age, aren't you?"

"I'm twenty-two," she announced proudly, taking my arm like Judy Garland latched onto the Cowardly Lion. "Well, if we're going to have to wait a while, I guess one drink wouldn't hurt. Lead the way!"

We stepped inside the terminal and walked to the end of the building where the new Conch Flyer was located. I had been coming here since the late seventies, not because I like to fly, which I don't but because the bar didn't have to adhere to the city law that mandated all bars have to be closed at four a.m. Between four and seven it was the only game in town. Aside from being a popular watering hole, The Conch Flyer became the hangout of the rich and famous that came and went through the Key West airport. Before the airport was renovated, the original Conch Flyer was also the only place at the airport that was air-conditioned, all the more reason to hang out while you were waiting for a flight or just wanted to drink late at night.

Nowadays the bar is open, clean, and airy, nothing like the lacquered wood, hand-carved model airplanes that used to adorn the ceiling and carpet on the floor that your shoes would stick to. We both climbed up on barstools, and I couldn't help but admire her long slender legs. I knew my conscience would keep this from going anywhere with this, but it was fun to leer. "Vodka cranberry," I ordered and turned to the model. "Oh, a Cosmopolitan, I guess." The bartender brought the drinks. "I propose a toast," I said. "To my return to Key West and to your first visit." I hesitated for a moment. "Hey, I don't even know your name." I stuck out my hand. "Russell," I offered.

"Brie." She accepted my handshake.

Sheesh. Why did Gen X'ers name their kids after cheese?

One drink led to another and by the time Rumpy showed, I had learned two things. One, Brie wasn't dumb. In fact, she was working on her Master's at Stetson College in Business Administration, and two, she was more than happy to cruise past her one-drink limit. Rumpy sat on the stool next to us, and over our protests, ordered another round, and then another. I was going to need some food to soak up this vodka, and Brie was getting way too drunk, way too attractive, and way too friendly. Halfway through the next round, Rumpy excused himself to use the men's room. When he was out of sight, Brie leaned over to me and said in a slur. "Can I tell you a secret? You look like someone who can keep a secret." (*Baby you don't know the half of it.*) I acknowledged that she could put me in her confidence and then she dropped the bombshell. "I'm gonna win this pageant, and after I do, I'm going to announce to the world that I'm the first Transsexual Miss Key West." She giggled, "Isn't that just precious?"

After almost spraying my drink all over the bar, I took it all in. Living in Key West all my life, nothing should have surprised me. I had met all manners of gays, crossdressers, transsexuals, and any other combination possible. Almost all of them were kind, friendly, and respected me. That wasn't my persuasion, but I certainly didn't have an aversion to befriending someone who was. I picked up the conversation like we were discussing what kind of bait to use for sailfish.

"So, you had reassignment surgery?" I asked.

"Not yet, just hormone shots to enhance my breasts and impede facial hair growth, and the five-thousand-dollar first prize in this contest won't be a drop in the bucket toward my goal, but it's a start." I nodded sagely. Looking carefully now at the face and the body, I could see now she was a man, although a very pretty one.

"So, are you attracted to men or women?" I asked further.

"Oh, I like boys. Straight boys," she answered. If I play my cards right I can go from cocktails to breakfast and they never find out who they are playing with." She wiggled with excitement. That's the fun of it all."

About then Rumpy returned from the men's room and Brie exclaimed. "My turn," and slid off the barstool, the mini skirt sliding almost up to her ass. Careful there girl, I thought to myself or your secret won't be a secret anymore. She wobbled away on her stiletto heels. I turned to Rumpy and explained. "I was looking for accommodations, hopefully, long term, but you have apparently offered your spare room tonight to yon princess." I nodded toward the ladies' room. "When we leave here, you can just drop me off at the Doubletree, and we can talk about renting your room by the month tomorrow."

"Are you kidding, pal?" He answered, pointing toward Brie. "There's a twenty-something bombshell contestant in there, full of distilled grain beverage bravery and my spare bedroom is unexpectedly occupied. I'll bet you twenty bucks she will end up in the sack with me if we play this right. *Capeche*?"

I started to explain how that might not turn out as he expected and then came to my diabolical senses.

"I'll do what I can to make your wishes come through," I said solemnly. "In fact, based on what I learned before you got here, I predict you're about to score a world-class blow job followed by the best anal sex imaginable."

After a few more drinks, we all walked arm in arm toward the door. Rumpy had the biggest shit-eatin' grin you ever saw.

For that matter, so did Brie.

25
Finders Keepers

Santos Galarza, a distant decedent of the Galarza family who had been a part of Cuban aristocracy for over three hundred years, was a day laborer and was hired as part of the clean-up crew at the old, burned-out mansion. Coming ashore twenty miles from Key West in a makeshift wooden boat with an ancient Ford straight six motor for power, he chose to remain an illegal alien instead of applying for wet foot/dry foot political asylum status. So jobs paying cash and under the table were all he could seek. It was straightforward, but backbreaking work. Today, it was load the scorched timbers and burnt trash into the dumpster. Everything was burned out, except for the old cookroom. Surrounded by creosote-soaked railroad ties, built to protect the house, the old kitchen stood while the rest of the mansion was destroyed. With a crowbar and a shovel, he pried the walls apart and then ripped up the ancient floor. Keeping an eye for anything he might salvage and sell, he gathered some old lead pipe and found a length of copper wire jutting out of a newer portion.

All the metal sinks and fixtures were melted into useless slag but still might sell for a few dollars in Opa Locka, where a distant cousin worked at a scrapyard. Then he saw something glisten when he turned over some burned boards in the charred rubble. He reached down and picked up the item. He stared at the large gold cross, adorned with enormous jewels, partially melted and covered in what appeared to be dried blood. He glanced around for any witnesses. Seeing nobody else around, he slipped the cross into his pocket and continued his demolition work until late in the afternoon, when he furtively slipped away. He didn't notice the shimmering transparent shadow of a woman in a green silk dress drift along behind him down the street.

He left Key West that night aboard the Greyhound bus, fearing his treasure might be discovered. Santos drifted through Miami for a few weeks, sleeping on the beach and taking the handouts at local soup kitchens for the homeless. Nearly starving, he finally found a day job from an elderly Cuban *Patron*, who managed the grey-area shipping business along the Miami River, where illicit drug trade flowed freely, and illegal aliens could work for cash with little fear of deportation. Santos was terrified the heavy stolen cross would be discovered, so he approached the dock boss.

With hat in hand, he broached the boss with an opportunity. In Spanish he spoke; "Señor, I found an item a few weeks ago that may have some value. Can I show it to you and maybe sell it?" The old man, sitting in a metal folding chair and smoking a cigar, took the lighted *Cohiba* out of his mouth and waived permission, in a thick cloud of smoke. Pulling the necklace out of his shirt, he handed the cross to his boss. "What might it be worth to you?" he asked. The *Patron* held the artifact and turned it over carefully, noting the bloodstains and the melted metal. He felt its weight and suspected it could be real. He casually tossed it back to Santos. "Costume jewelry," he announced. "Worthless. It might be something my granddaughter can put on her dolls." He reached back for the cross. "Tell you what," he said nonchalantly. "You have been a good worker. I'll give you twenty dollars. Here."

Santos was crestfallen. He felt the cross was worth far more than that, but twenty dollars would let him survive a few more days.

"I appreciate your generosity, Señor," Santos answered, carefully replacing the cross around his neck, "But it's worth more as a good luck charm to me than twenty dollars. Gracias, but I'll keep it for now."

The boss held up two hands in a 'stop' motion, knowing the cross was worth far me. "Un-momento, Santos, let me look at it again. Perhaps I was hasty." He held out his hands toward the laborer for the cross, but Santos got suspicious now. Bowing in respect, he smiled, backed away, and turned. "Perhaps mañana, Señor. I will be here in the morning. By then I may be hungry enough to take twenty-five dollars." The Patron nodded in agreement. By tomorrow, he thought he could pay some of his crew to murder the little Cuban and take the cross, undoubtedly worth thousands or more, away from his dead body. But Santos had other ideas at that point. That evening, at closing time, he failed to put the keys away on one of the company trucks. Quietly sliding behind the wheel after dark, he turned on the ignition and smiled with satisfaction when he saw the gas gauge move to the "full" mark. Sitting quietly until nobody was around; he started the truck, shifted the gear shift to "drive" and quietly motored out of the driveway. Having learned to drive from his uncle in Havana, in a fifty-year-old Ford, this truck seemed at first strange without a clutch pedal, but in a few minutes, the automatic transmission became familiar. Driving west away from the polluted Miami River, he caught the first onramp to US95. He thought to himself. Here I am, an illegal alien in a foreign country, two dollars to my name, driving a stolen truck. He rolled down the window and laughed out loud to the world.

"La Vida trans es una Aventura!" Life is an adventure!

How far will a full tank take me? Having no idea where to go, Santos drove north on Highway 95 until the truck indicated less than a quarter tank. Taking the next exit at Vero Beach, he crossed the Indian River causeway and turned north on A1A. Fifteen minutes later, the gas gage on empty, the truck chugged to a halt near Sebastian Inlet State Park. Abanding the stolen dead truck, he put the gold cross around his neck and strung his shoes over his shoulders.

Santos walked to the lonely beach and sat down on a limestone outcropping that once resembled a horse's head, just yards from where nearly fifteen hundred sailors lay shipwrecked four hundred years earlier. Oblivious to the history, he sat in the dark until nearly sunrise. With a sigh he removed the heavy cross from his neck, he scooped out a deep hole, stopping when he felt a hard bottom, not realizing he had touched a hundred thousand dollars worth of silver pieces of eight, hidden so long before by the shipwrecked sailors, nonferrous undetectable by any device. Laying the cross in the bottom of the hole, he said a silent prayer to himself, muttering that he would hide the cross here until he could find someone who recognized its real value.

"Why do you hide my cross, cousin?" a voice asked. "You are my cousin, aren't you? I sense it." Santos never heard the last part of Louisa's sentence. He was already fifty yards down the beach, shoes abandoned, cross forgotten, running in terror from the unattached voice, despite the soft beach sand.

26
A Boy And His Toys

Ever since he learned he was accidentally named after a famous pirate, nine-year-old Billy Kidd became obsessed with treasure, shipwrecks, and swashbuckling adventures. When the annual family vacation centered on Disney World and Florida, Ohio-born Billy wasn't excited about a visit to the magic kingdom but hounded his mom and dad incessantly for a side trip to the Treasure Coast and a metal detector for Christmas so he could find millions in buried treasure.

"Those beaches have been combed over by thousands of people," Billy's father cautioned. "You could look for days and never find more than a rusty can. It's a waste of time."

But Billy was unrelenting, pestering his parents morning, noon, and night, and screamed with delight on Christmas Day when he unwrapped a Bounty Hunter metal detector. Purchased at Harbor Freight for $64.99, it was the cheapest detector on the market. While marginally effective, it would suffice to let Billy wear himself out in the soft sand, combing Sebastian Beach one afternoon.

Most young boys would treasure a visit to Disneyworld and Universal Studios, but he could hardly contain himself, obsessed with his beach visit. Finally, after five days of standing in long lines, riding rides, and standing for pictures with characters in costumes with his little sister, Finally, the day came for the trip to the beach, coincidentally only a week after Santos had the unexpected visit from his distant Cuban cousin on that very beach.

While his mom, dad, and sister huddled in the sand under a big umbrella, Billy began his lon-practiced sweep of the beach. As his father predicted, Billy trudged through the deep sand, lugging the detector and sweeping back and forth, a procedure he had read and seen in countless treasure magazines. Despite the lightweight device, the cheap detector was an armful for a nine-year-old boy, and after two hours, he was hot, exhausted, and discouraged.

Taking a break under the umbrella. Billy's father pointed up the beach, well above the high tide level, almost where the sand met the sea oats. "Why don't you try up there?" His father suggested.

“I bet that area doesn’t get as much action as the beach.

Looking up at the sand and knowing the dry dunes would be even harder to walk on, subsequently wearing him out in minutes so they could return to the resort and the pool, Billy dragged himself to his feet and drugged off toward the dunes. His father stood up. “I’ll walk with you, son, We can get rich together then.”

Barely able to walk in the soft sand, Billy swept the cheap detector back and forth. Far from his dreams of finding endless treasure with every sweep of the device, the effort was backbreaking and exhausting.

He was about to hand the detector to his father and give up when they approached a coral rock, an outcropping that resembled a horse head over three hundred years ago. Rain, storms, and wind had eroded it down to an unrecognizable lump. “This isn’t as easy as I thought it would be,” admitted the young boy. “I think I’m done looking for treasure.”

Before handing the detector to his father, he made one last future sweep to his left.

WHEEP!

27
Epilogue

The crunch of tires on gravel was hidden by Rude Girl's morning radio show as the black SUV pulled up in front of Rumpy's house. Bric was in the kitchen, preparing a breakfast quiche and he never heard the figure quietly step onto the porch and through the unlocked door to the kitchen. As Bric sensed the motion, he saw the barrel of a thirty eight automatic pointing at him. He hesitated for an instant as he recognized his assailant, but that was just long enough to have the room erupt in a deafening noise as three slugs pounded into him from less than ten feet. The shots slammed him into the cupboards with crushing force.

Bric staggered forward, and almost by instinct, pulled a cleaver from the butcher block holder. With one last effort, he heaved the cleaver at his assailant's head, splitting the skull almost all the way to the neck. Bric never made a sound and slowly slumped to the floor in a pool of blood, just a few feet from his dead assailant.

Also Available on Amazon By Wayne Gales

Treasure Key
Key West Camoflauge
A Normal Key West
Anybody's Bar in Key West
Southernmost Exposure
Southernmost Son
Bone Island Bodies
Once Upon a time in Key West
Living and Dying in Key West Time
The last three books available on Audible as a Trilogy

Cooking for the Hearing Impaired

Children's books, Illustrated by Lori Kus

We Wish to Fish
Sun, Sand, and the Salty Sea
Caught No Fish